Cinco
Puntos
Press

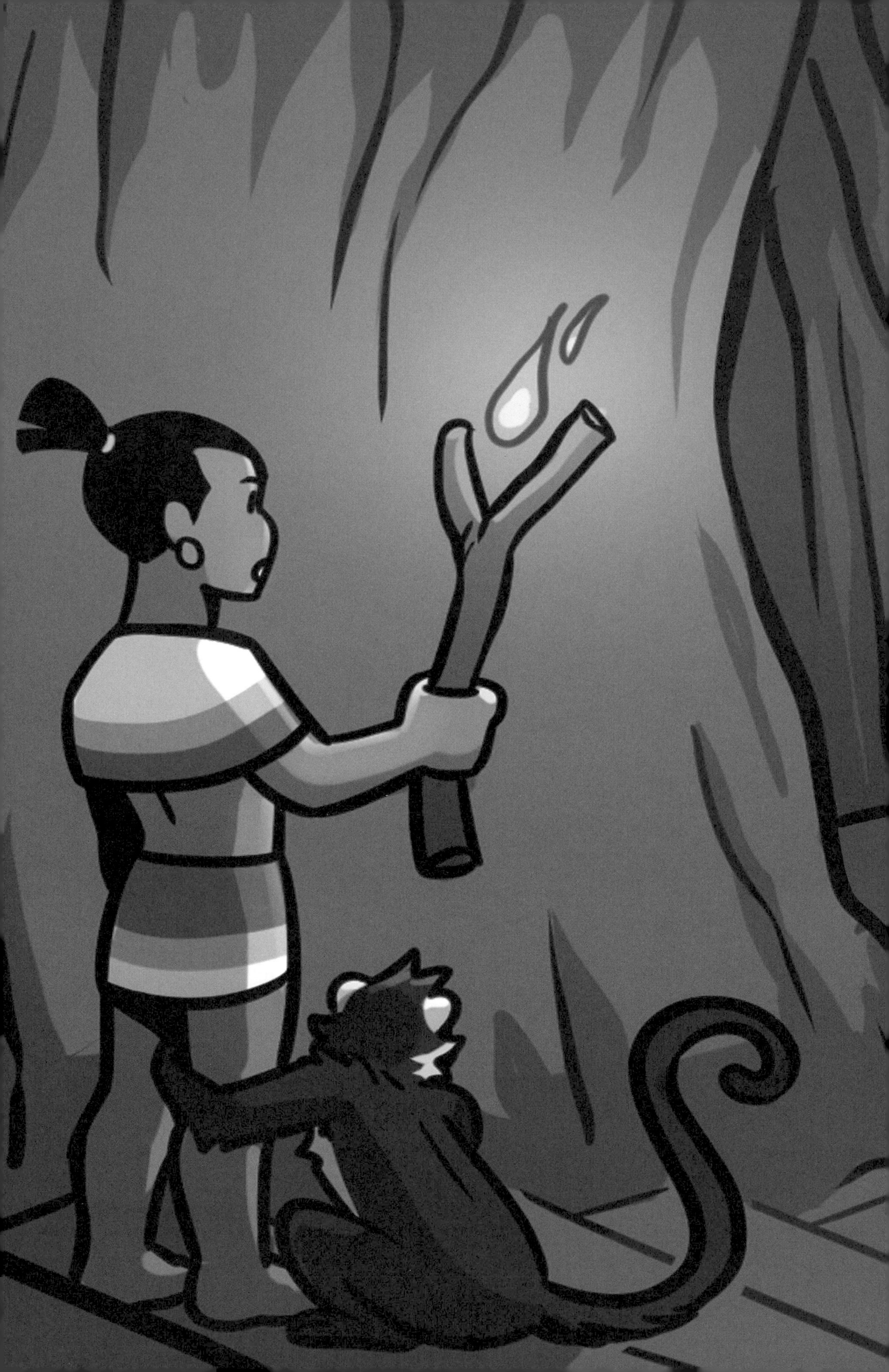

TALES OF THE
FEATHERED
SERPENT

by **David Bowles**

illustrated by
Charlene Bowles

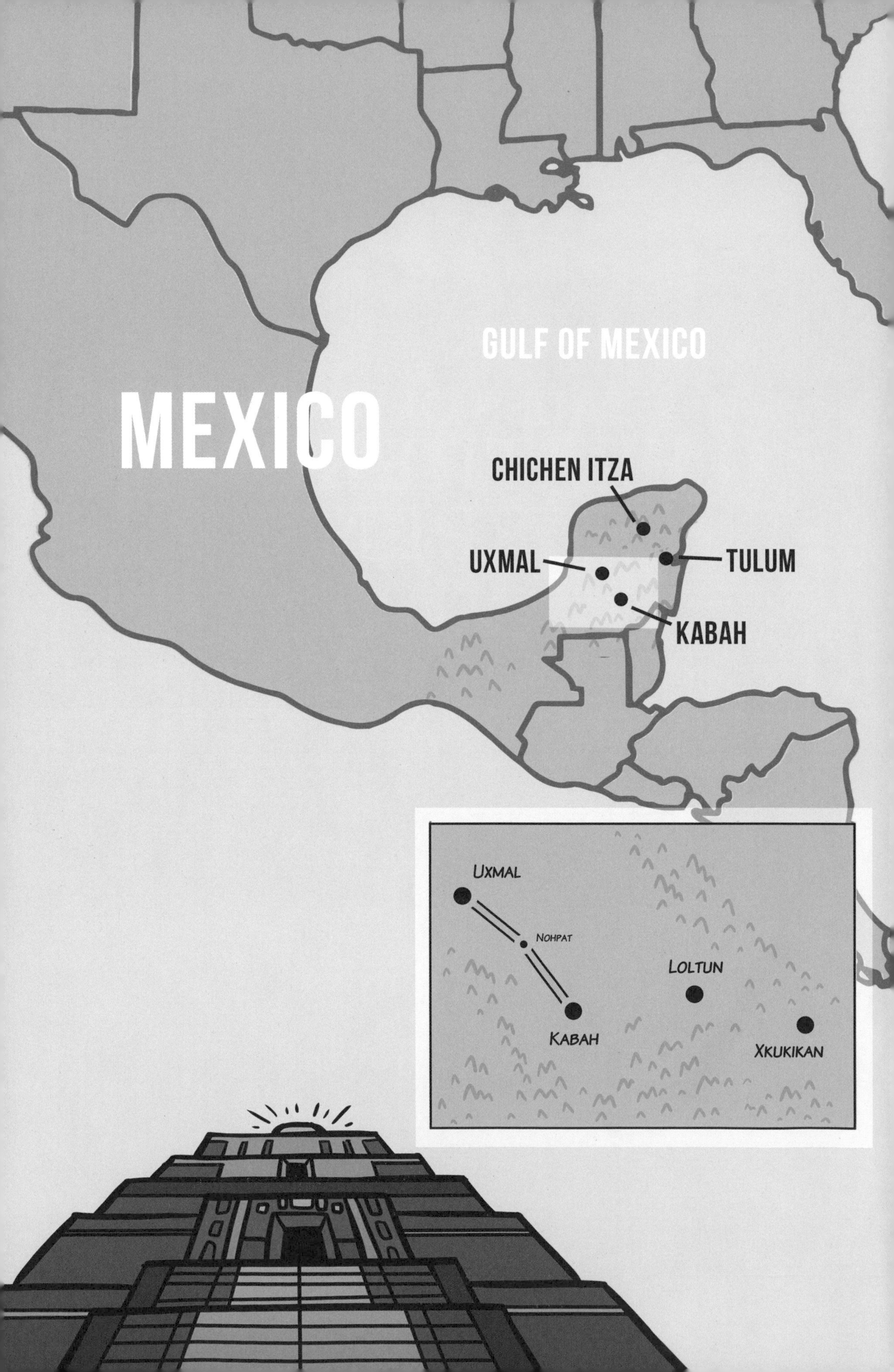

GULF OF MEXICO
MEXICO
CHICHEN ITZA
UXMAL
TULUM
KABAH
UXMAL
NOHPAT
LOLTUN
KABAH
XKUKIKAN

ALMAH
THE WITCH OF KABAH

Trained since she was young to be a healer for her people, Almah is
selected by the aluxes for a very special task: raising Sayam.

SAYAM
THE HALFLING BOY

Able to speak the moment he hatches from an egg, this fun-loving
and kind halfling boy was created by the aluxes to bring peace.

KINICH KAK EK
THE KING OF UXMAL

The first king of Uxmal in a hundred years, Kinich Kak Ek is an
ambitious and cruel man who will let nothing stand in his way.

ZAATAN IK
THE CHIEF SORCERER

Knowledgeable in all the dark arts, this wizard helped put Kinich Kak
Ek on the throne, but he would much rather unleash chaos.

MAAX
A CLEVER SPIDER MONKEY

Smart and agile, spider monkeys were revered by the Maya. Maax is
one of the smartest, if not all that agile.

CHULUL
LEADER OF THE ELFIN ALUXES

When humans arrived, aluxes retreated into jungles and caves, led by
wise ones like Chulul. She watches humanity, hopeful.

LOBIL
OLD SHAMAN OF THE ALUXES

The ancient aluxes have great magical lore. Lobil has lived thousands
of years and remembers it all.

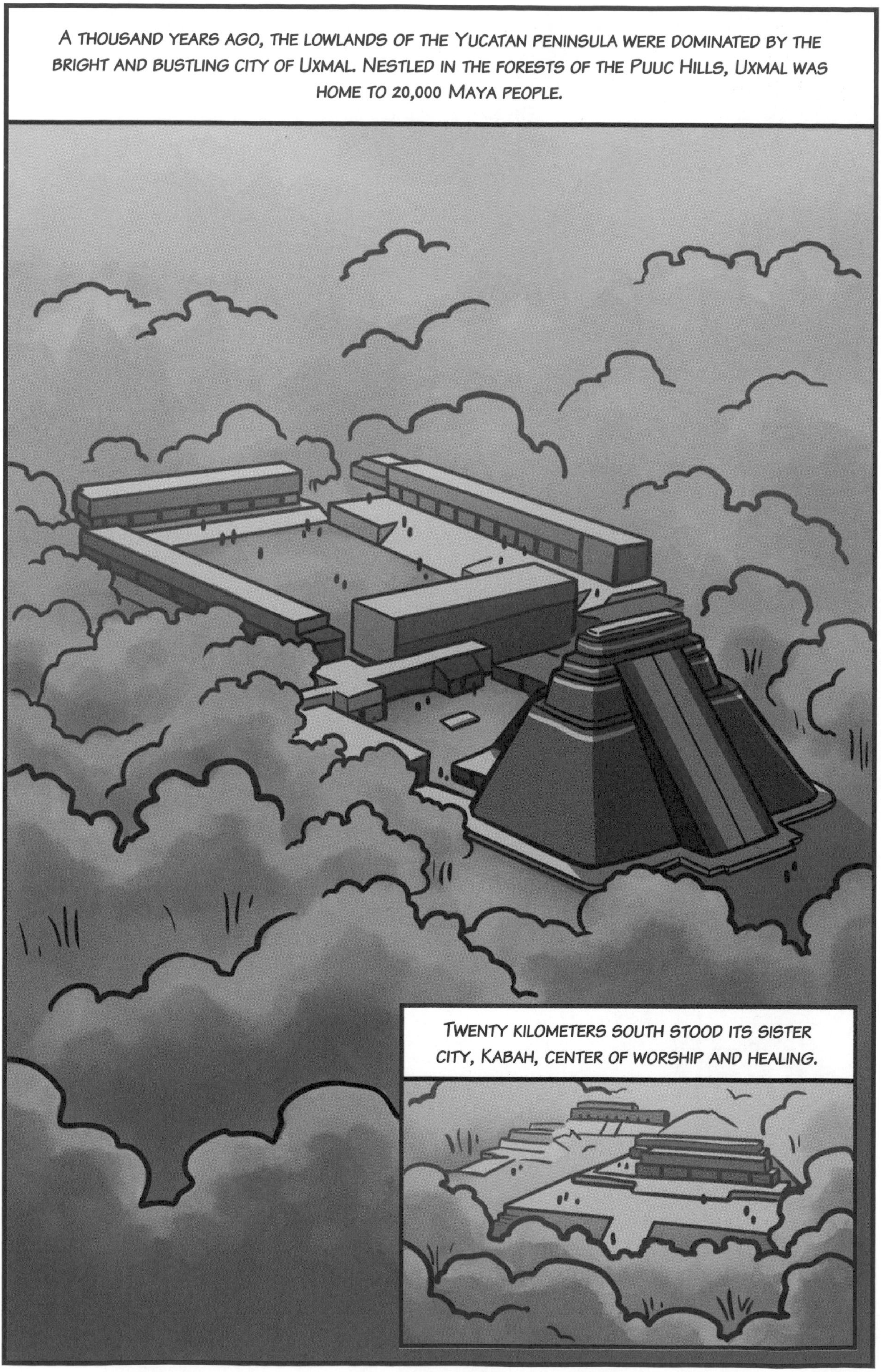
A THOUSAND YEARS AGO, THE LOWLANDS OF THE YUCATAN PENINSULA WERE DOMINATED BY THE BRIGHT AND BUSTLING CITY OF UXMAL. NESTLED IN THE FORESTS OF THE PUUC HILLS, UXMAL WAS HOME TO 20,000 MAYA PEOPLE.
TWENTY KILOMETERS SOUTH STOOD ITS SISTER CITY, KABAH, CENTER OF WORSHIP AND HEALING.

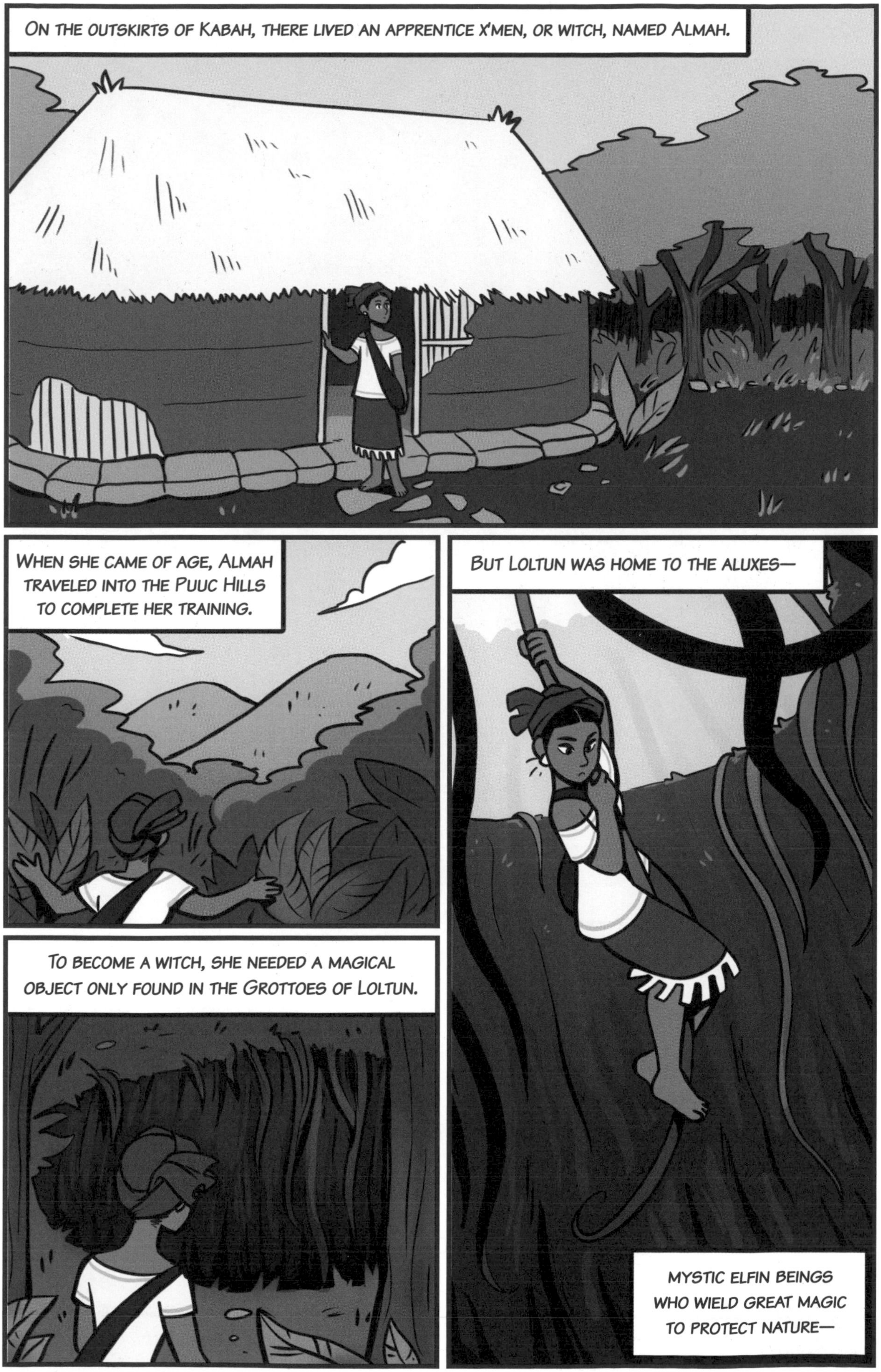
On the outskirts of Kabah, there lived an apprentice x'men, or witch, named Almah.
When she came of age, Almah traveled into the Puuc Hills to complete her training.
To become a witch, she needed a magical object only found in the Grottoes of Loltun.
But Loltun was home to the aluxes—
Mystic elfin beings who wield great magic to protect nature—

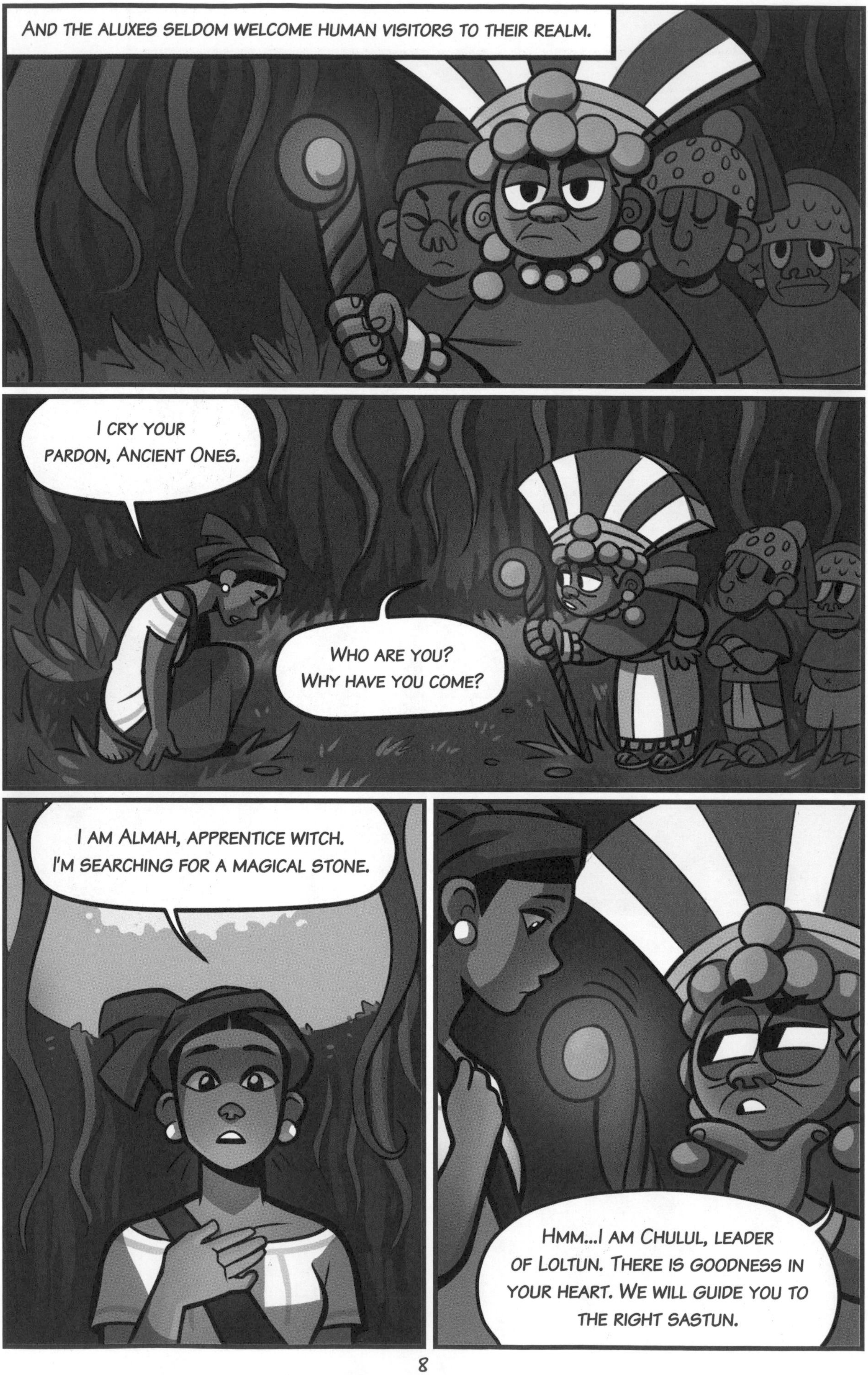
AND THE ALUXES SELDOM WELCOME HUMAN VISITORS TO THEIR REALM.
I CRY YOUR PARDON, ANCIENT ONES.
WHO ARE YOU? WHY HAVE YOU COME?
I AM ALMAH, APPRENTICE WITCH. I'M SEARCHING FOR A MAGICAL STONE.
HMM...I AM CHULUL, LEADER OF LOLTUN. THERE IS GOODNESS IN YOUR HEART. WE WILL GUIDE YOU TO THE RIGHT SASTUN.

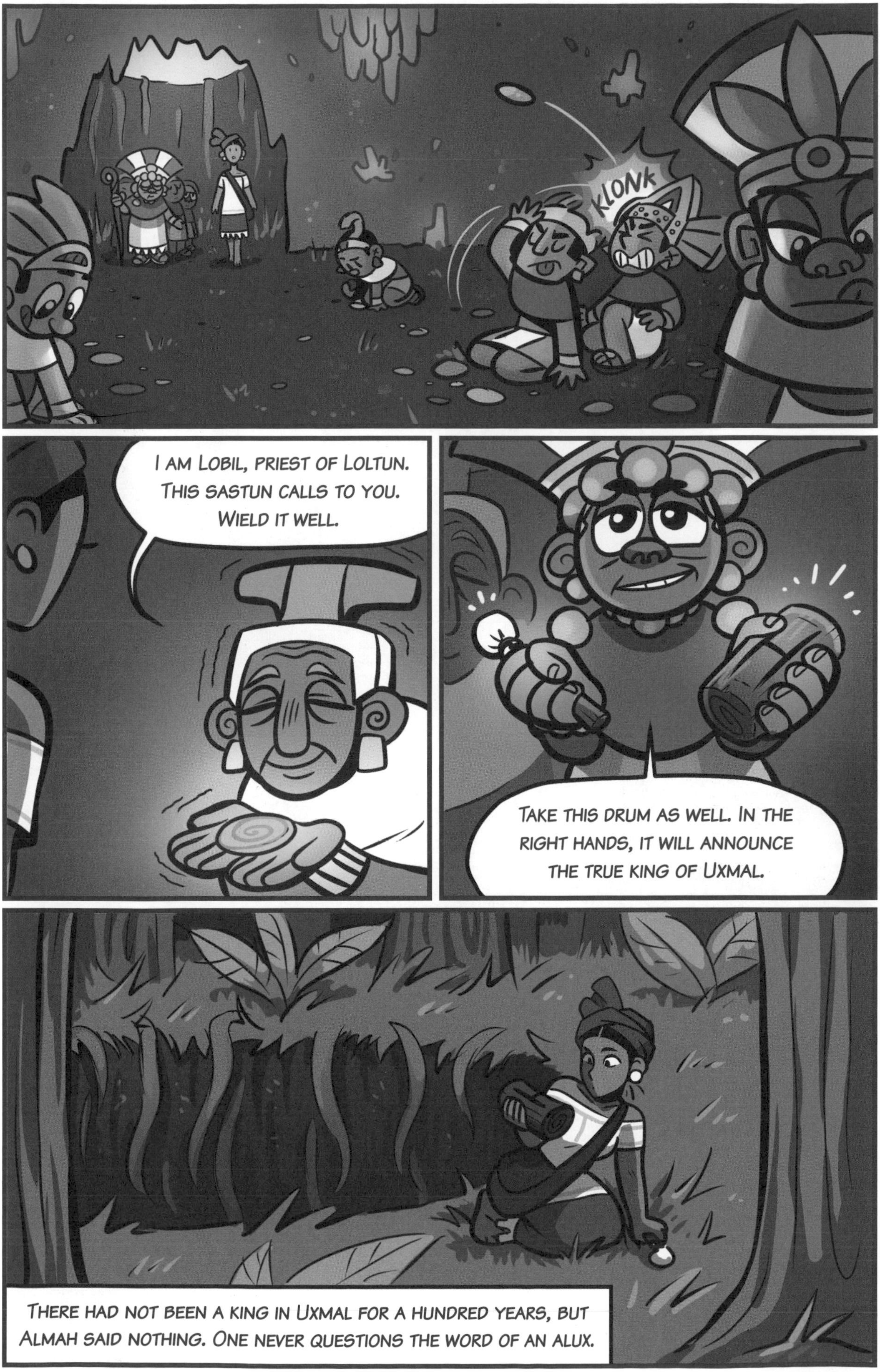
KLONK
I AM LOBIL, PRIEST OF LOLTUN. THIS SASTUN CALLS TO YOU. WIELD IT WELL.
TAKE THIS DRUM AS WELL. IN THE RIGHT HANDS, IT WILL ANNOUNCE THE TRUE KING OF UXMAL.
THERE HAD NOT BEEN A KING IN UXMAL FOR A HUNDRED YEARS, BUT ALMAH SAID NOTHING. ONE NEVER QUESTIONS THE WORD OF AN ALUX.

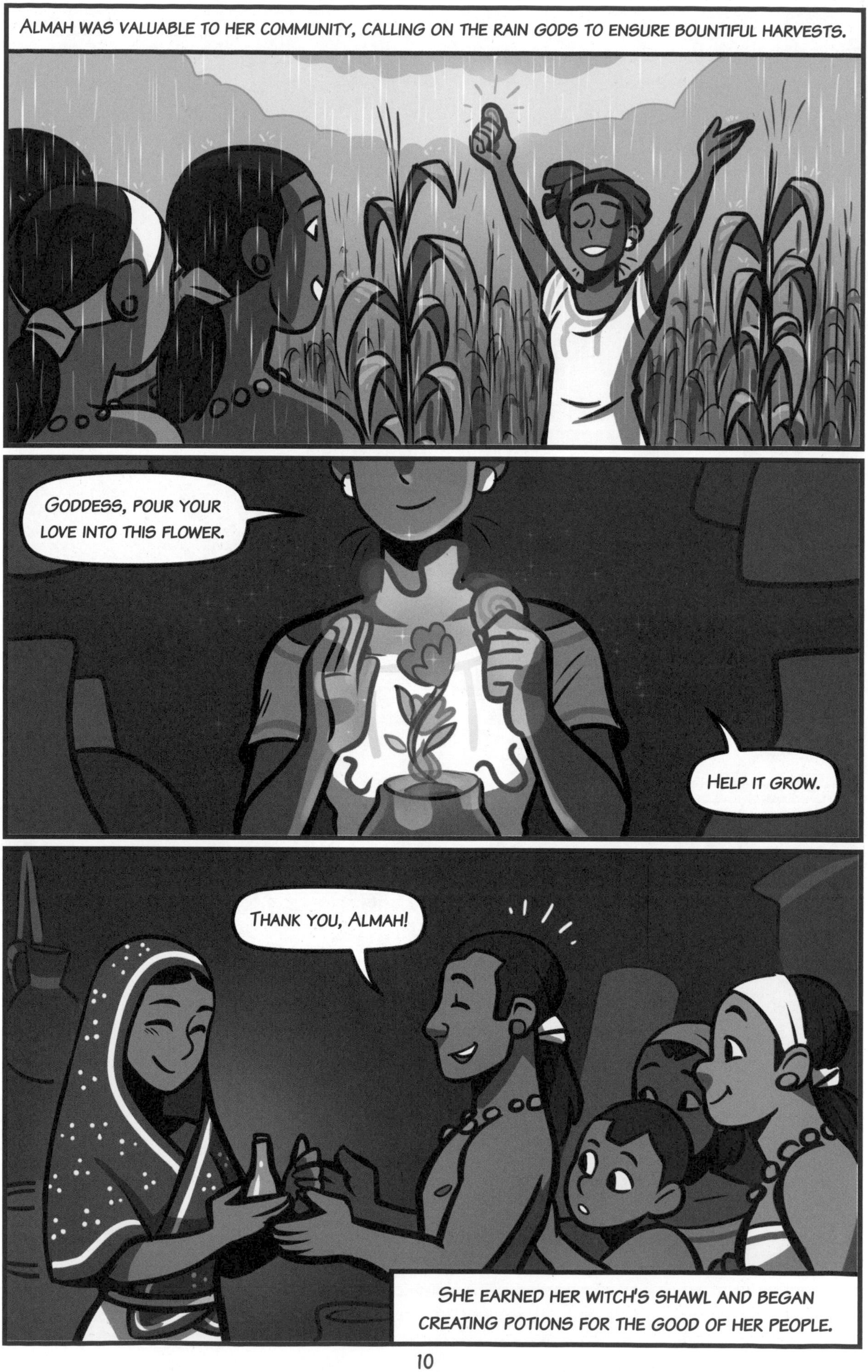
ALMAH WAS VALUABLE TO HER COMMUNITY, CALLING ON THE RAIN GODS TO ENSURE BOUNTIFUL HARVESTS.
GODDESS, POUR YOUR LOVE INTO THIS FLOWER.
HELP IT GROW.
THANK YOU, ALMAH!
SHE EARNED HER WITCH'S SHAWL AND BEGAN CREATING POTIONS FOR THE GOOD OF HER PEOPLE.

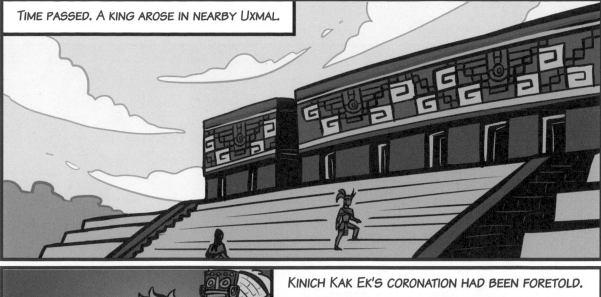

TIME PASSED. A KING AROSE IN NEARBY UXMAL.

KINICH KAK EK'S CORONATION HAD BEEN FORETOLD.

THE SORCERER ZAATAN IK, CHIEF ADVISOR, ANNOUNCED ANOTHER PROPHECY.

NO MAN BORN OF A WOMAN CAN USURP YOUR THRONE.

THERE IS MORE.

"WHEN THE KINGMAKER DRUM SETS THE KINGDOM A-THRUM, A RIVAL YOU MUST BEST WITH THREE IMPOSSIBLE TESTS."

A RIVAL?
NOT BORN?
KINGMAKER DRUM?
FOOLISHNESS!

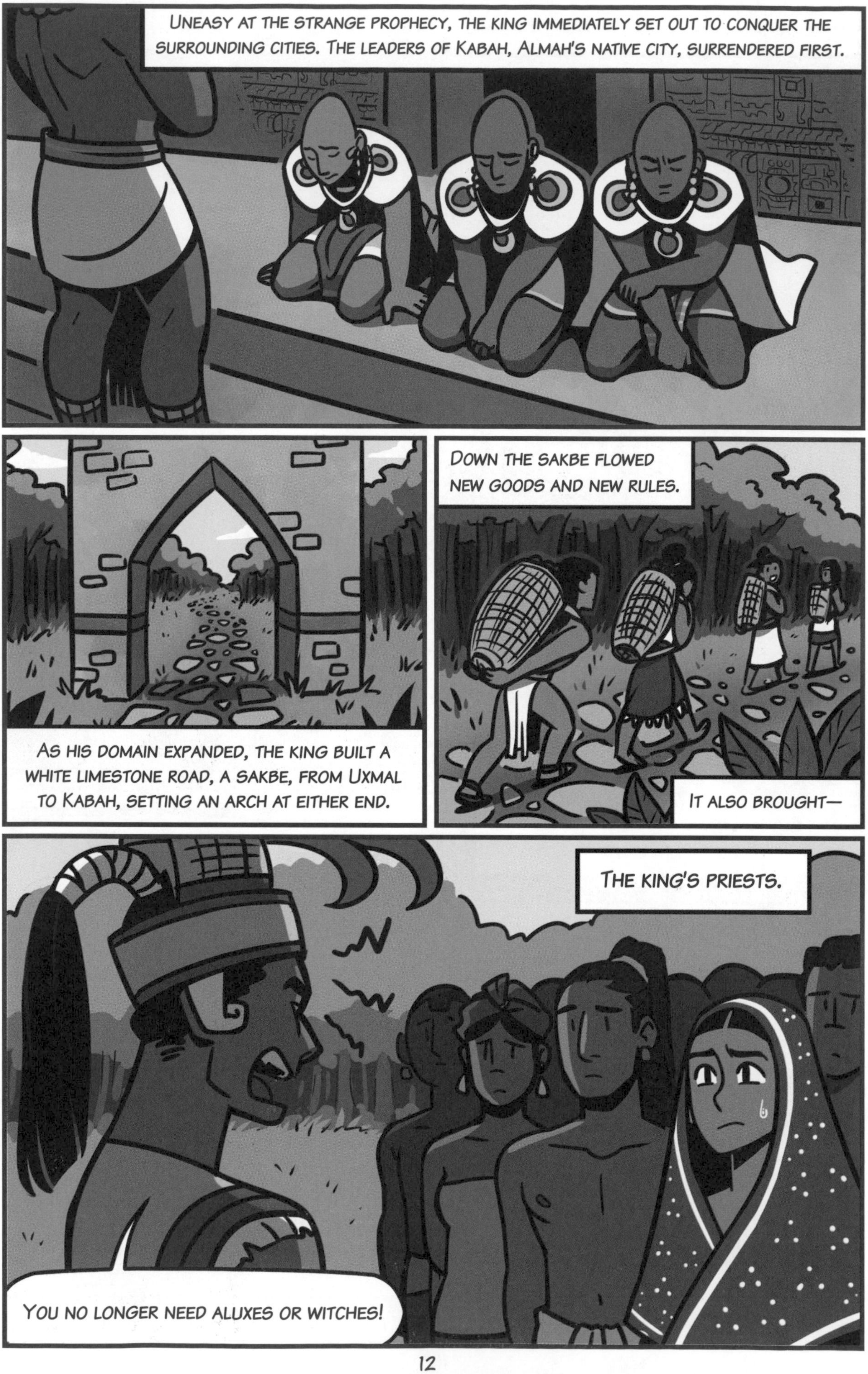
UNEASY AT THE STRANGE PROPHECY, THE KING IMMEDIATELY SET OUT TO CONQUER THE SURROUNDING CITIES. THE LEADERS OF KABAH, ALMAH'S NATIVE CITY, SURRENDERED FIRST.
AS HIS DOMAIN EXPANDED, THE KING BUILT A WHITE LIMESTONE ROAD, A SAKBE, FROM UXMAL TO KABAH, SETTING AN ARCH AT EITHER END.
DOWN THE SAKBE FLOWED NEW GOODS AND NEW RULES.
IT ALSO BROUGHT—
THE KING'S PRIESTS.
YOU NO LONGER NEED ALUXES OR WITCHES!

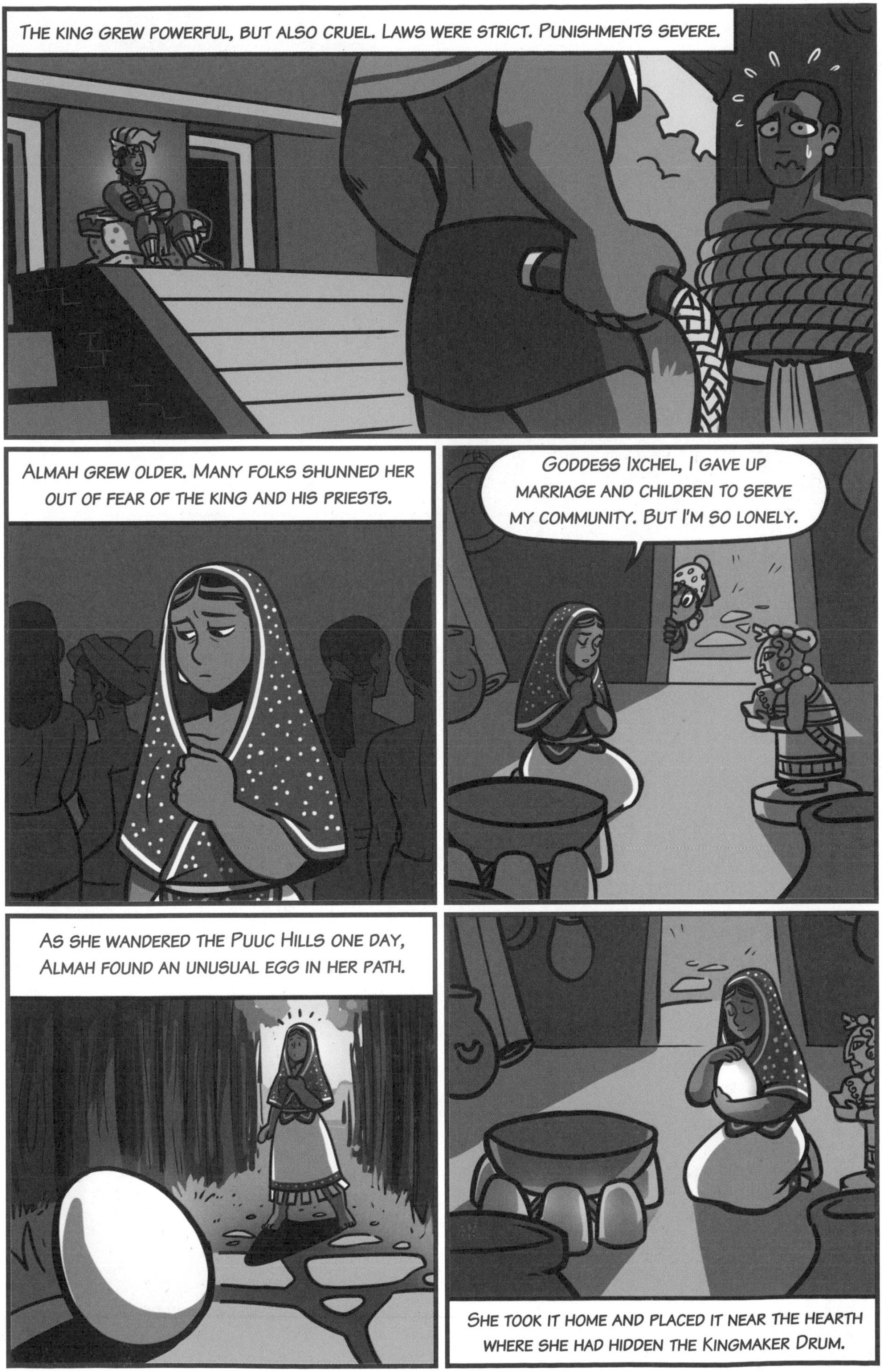
THE KING GREW POWERFUL, BUT ALSO CRUEL. LAWS WERE STRICT. PUNISHMENTS SEVERE.
ALMAH GREW OLDER. MANY FOLKS SHUNNED HER OUT OF FEAR OF THE KING AND HIS PRIESTS.
GODDESS IXCHEL, I GAVE UP MARRIAGE AND CHILDREN TO SERVE MY COMMUNITY. BUT I'M SO LONELY.
AS SHE WANDERED THE PUUC HILLS ONE DAY, ALMAH FOUND AN UNUSUAL EGG IN HER PATH.
SHE TOOK IT HOME AND PLACED IT NEAR THE HEARTH WHERE SHE HAD HIDDEN THE KINGMAKER DRUM.

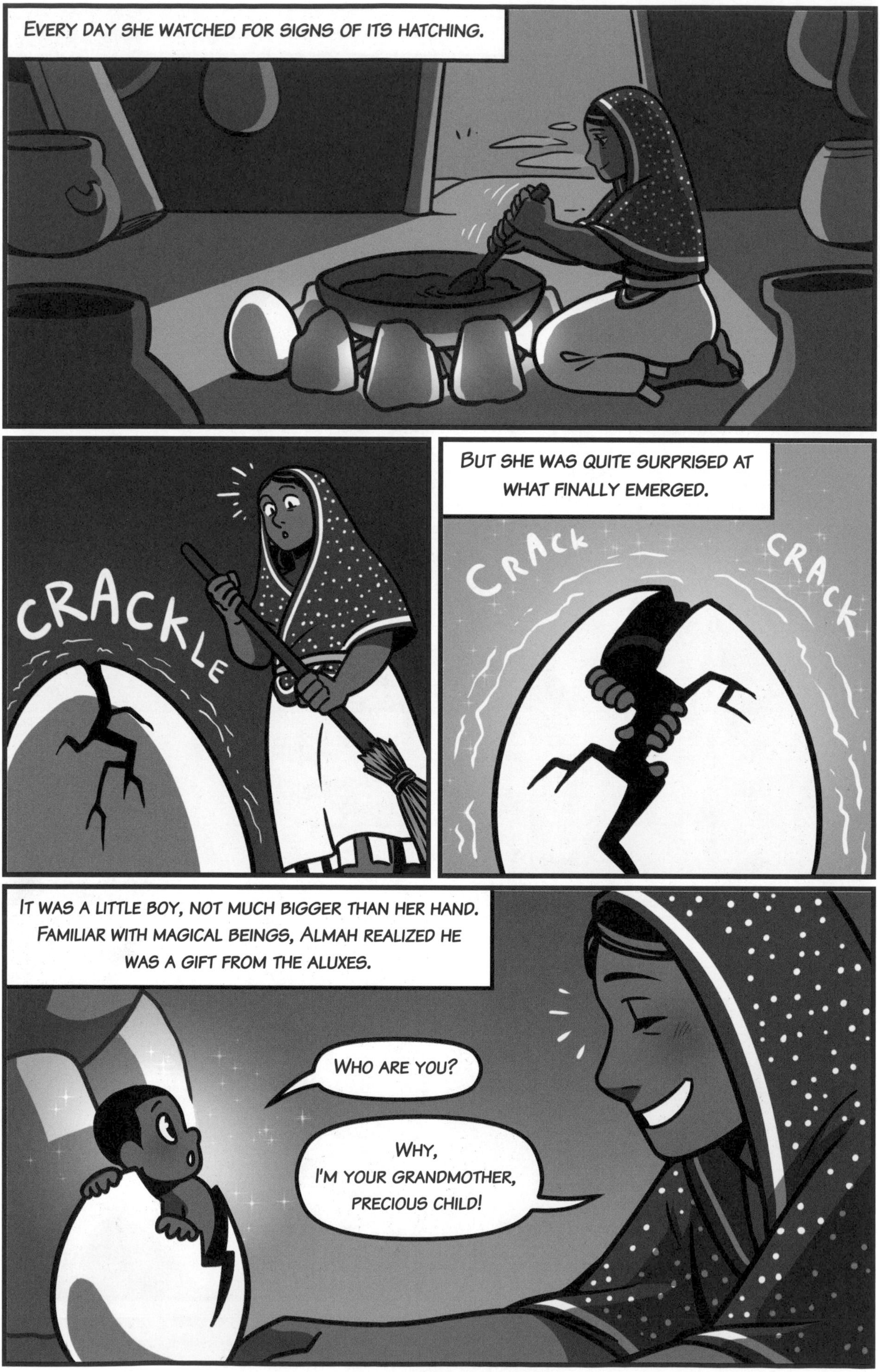
EVERY DAY SHE WATCHED FOR SIGNS OF ITS HATCHING.
CRACKLE
BUT SHE WAS QUITE SURPRISED AT WHAT FINALLY EMERGED.
CRACK
CRACK
IT WAS A LITTLE BOY, NOT MUCH BIGGER THAN HER HAND. FAMILIAR WITH MAGICAL BEINGS, ALMAH REALIZED HE WAS A GIFT FROM THE ALUXES.
WHO ARE YOU?
WHY, I'M YOUR GRANDMOTHER, PRECIOUS CHILD!

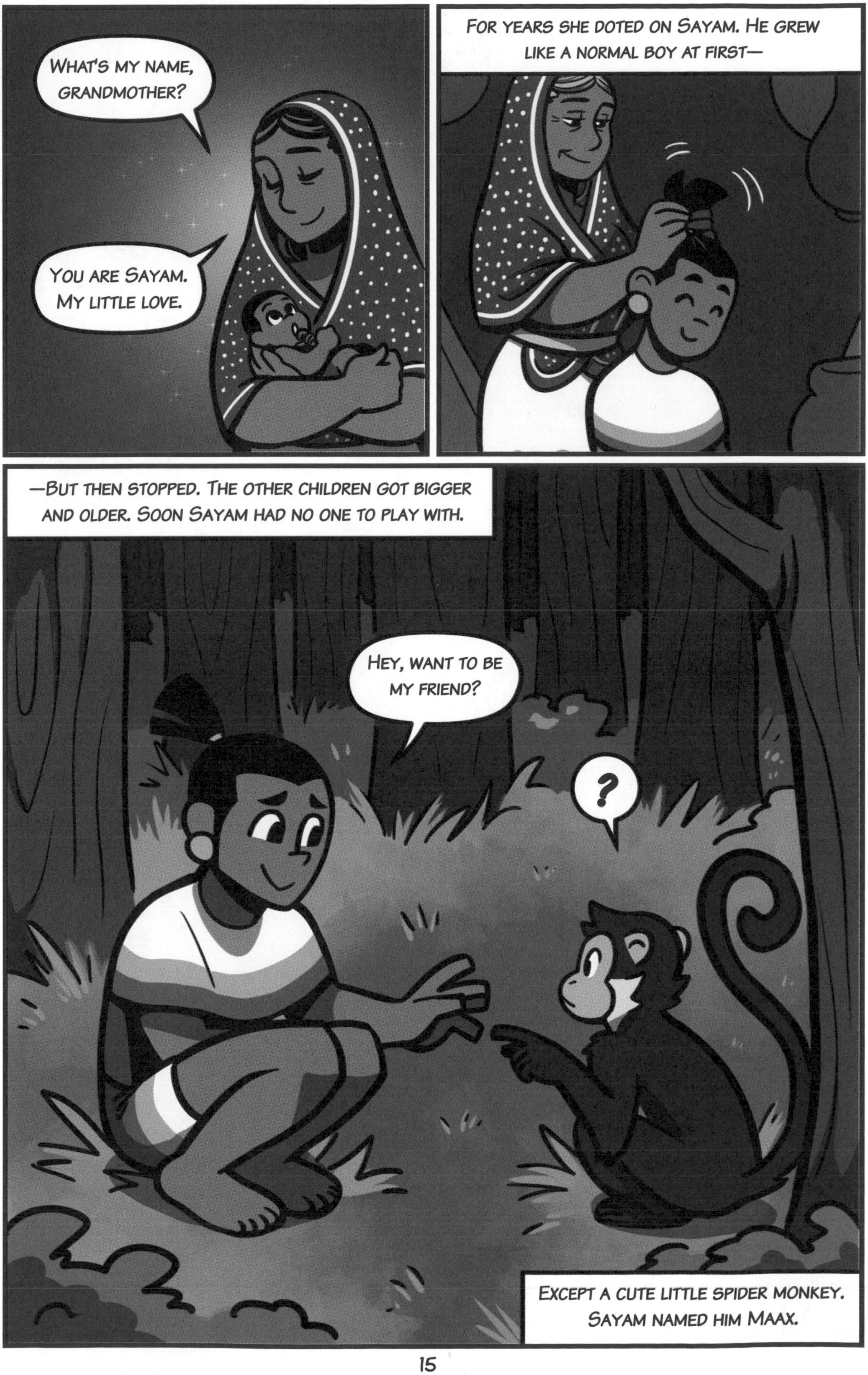

WHAT'S MY NAME, GRANDMOTHER?
YOU ARE SAYAM. MY LITTLE LOVE.
FOR YEARS SHE DOTED ON SAYAM. HE GREW LIKE A NORMAL BOY AT FIRST—
—BUT THEN STOPPED. THE OTHER CHILDREN GOT BIGGER AND OLDER. SOON SAYAM HAD NO ONE TO PLAY WITH.
HEY, WANT TO BE MY FRIEND?
?
EXCEPT A CUTE LITTLE SPIDER MONKEY. SAYAM NAMED HIM MAAX.

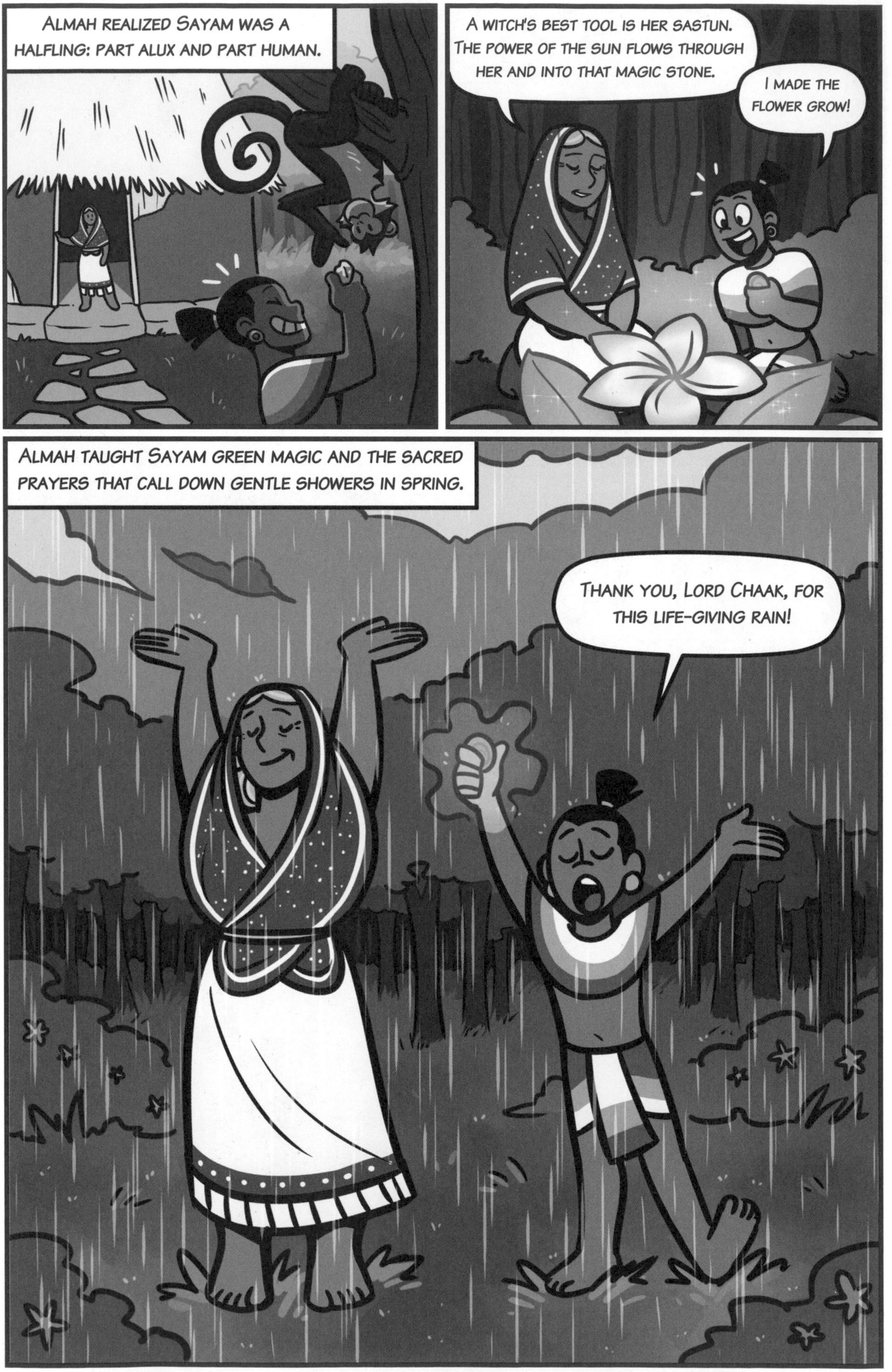
ALMAH REALIZED SAYAM WAS A HALFLING: PART ALUX AND PART HUMAN.
A WITCH'S BEST TOOL IS HER SASTUN. THE POWER OF THE SUN FLOWS THROUGH HER AND INTO THAT MAGIC STONE.
I MADE THE FLOWER GROW!
ALMAH TAUGHT SAYAM GREEN MAGIC AND THE SACRED PRAYERS THAT CALL DOWN GENTLE SHOWERS IN SPRING.
THANK YOU, LORD CHAAK, FOR THIS LIFE-GIVING RAIN!

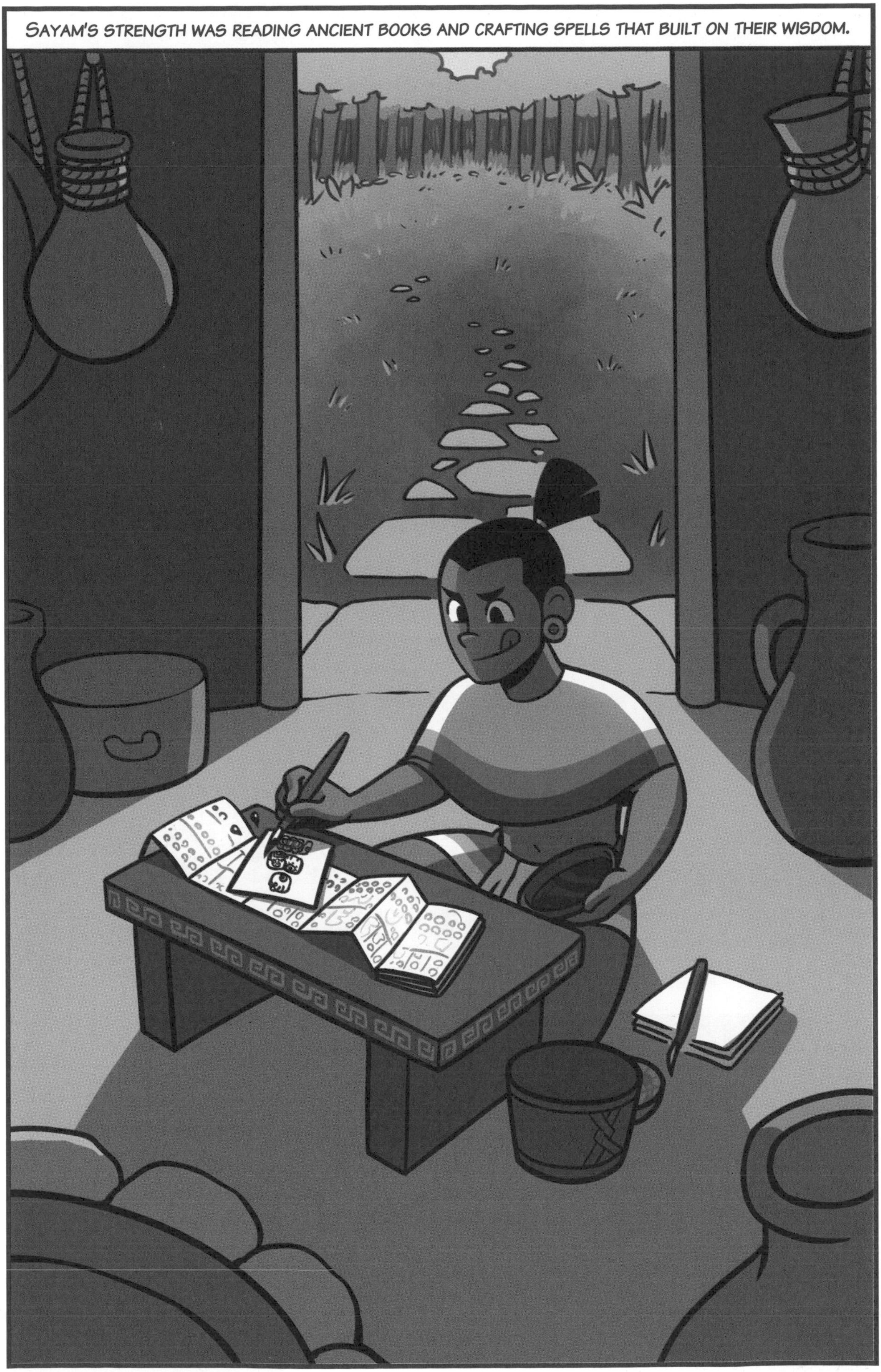
SAYAM'S STRENGTH WAS READING ANCIENT BOOKS AND CRAFTING SPELLS THAT BUILT ON THEIR WISDOM.

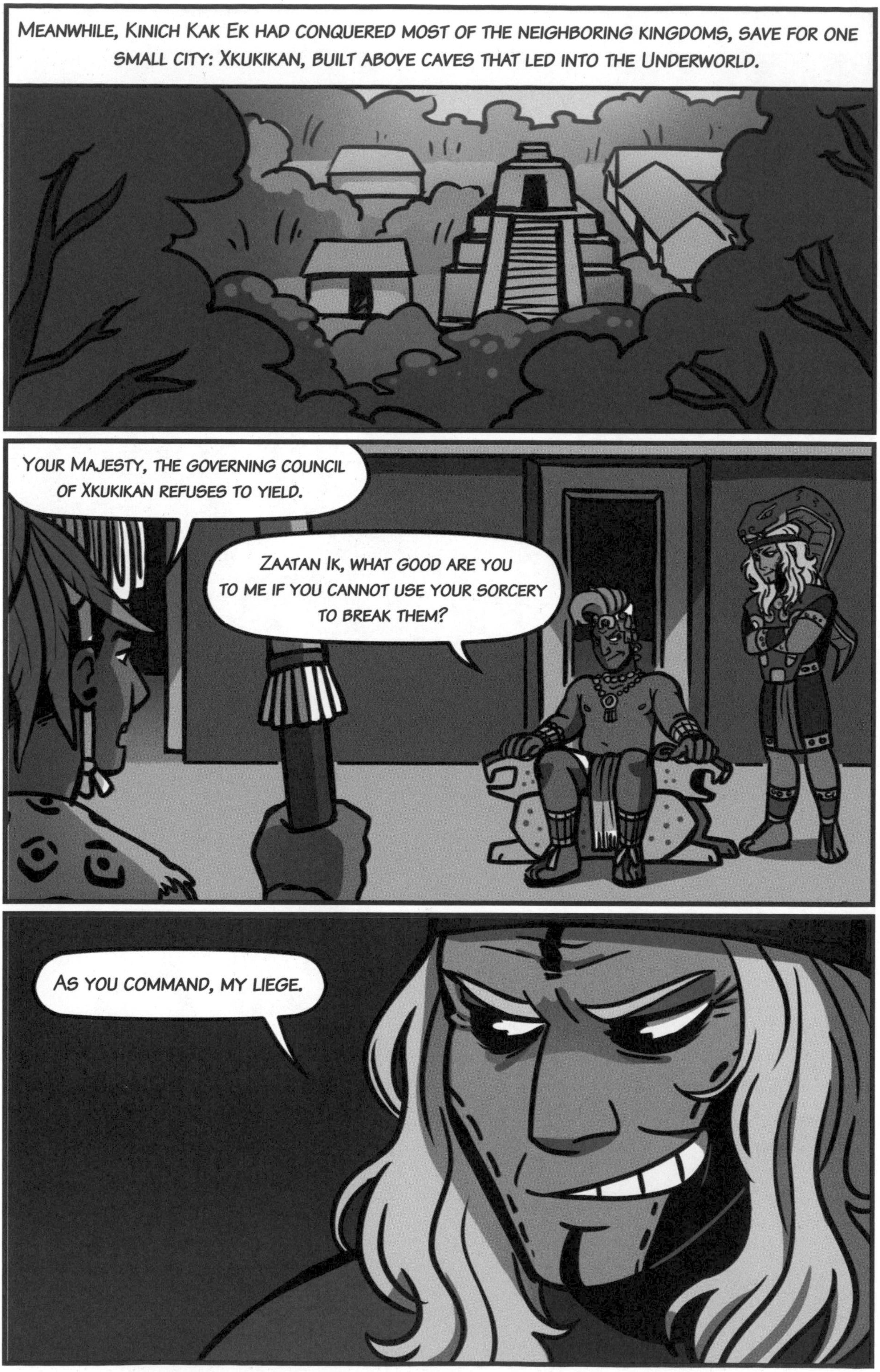
MEANWHILE, KINICH KAK EK HAD CONQUERED MOST OF THE NEIGHBORING KINGDOMS, SAVE FOR ONE SMALL CITY: XKUKIKAN, BUILT ABOVE CAVES THAT LED INTO THE UNDERWORLD.
YOUR MAJESTY, THE GOVERNING COUNCIL OF XKUKIKAN REFUSES TO YIELD.
ZAATAN IK, WHAT GOOD ARE YOU TO ME IF YOU CANNOT USE YOUR SORCERY TO BREAK THEM?
AS YOU COMMAND, MY LIEGE.

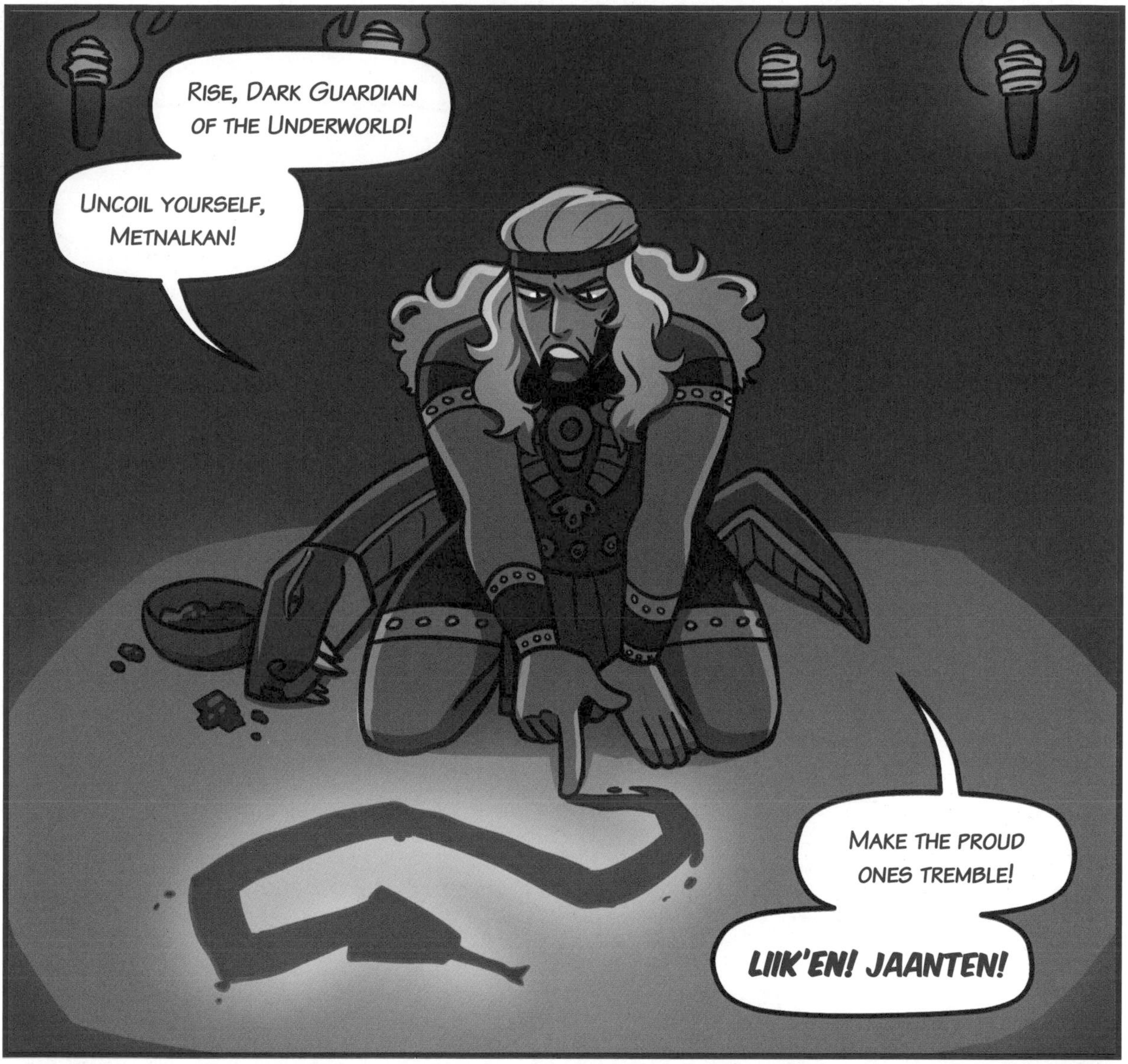
RISE, DARK GUARDIAN OF THE UNDERWORLD!
UNCOIL YOURSELF, METNALKAN!
MAKE THE PROUD ONES TREMBLE!
LIIK'EN! JAANTEN!

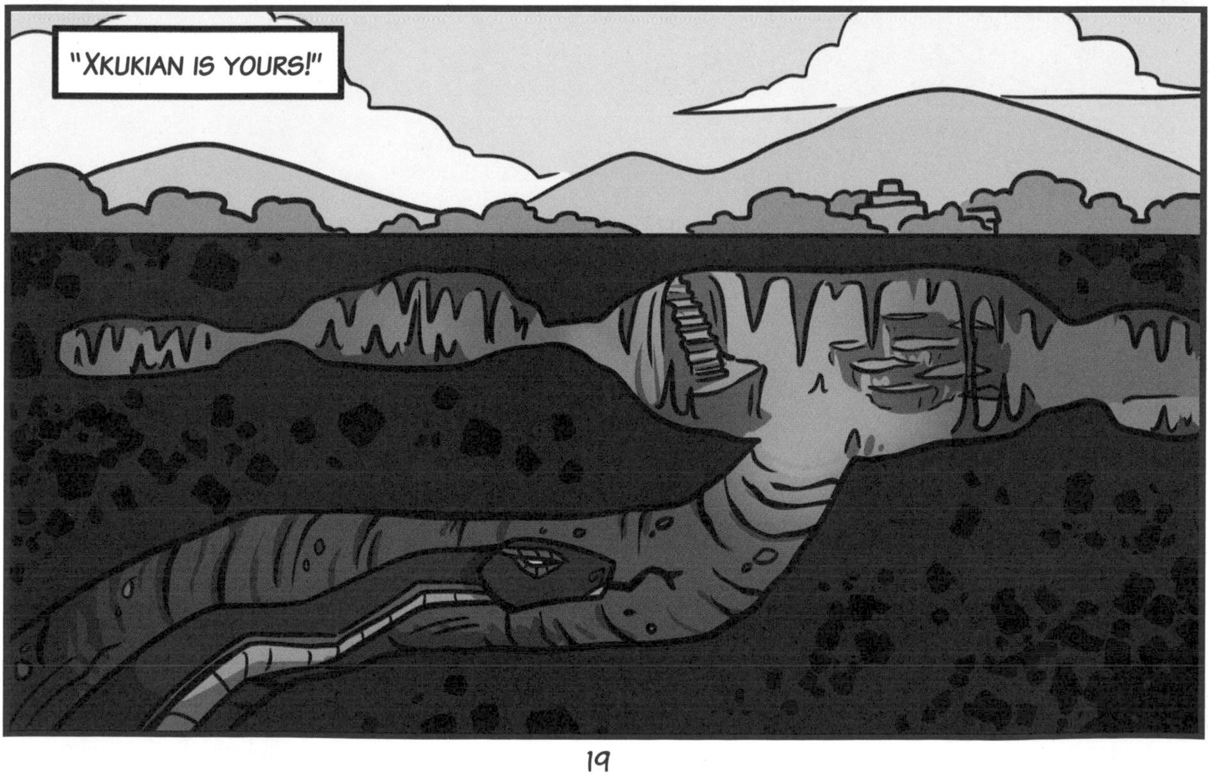
"XKUKIAN IS YOURS!"

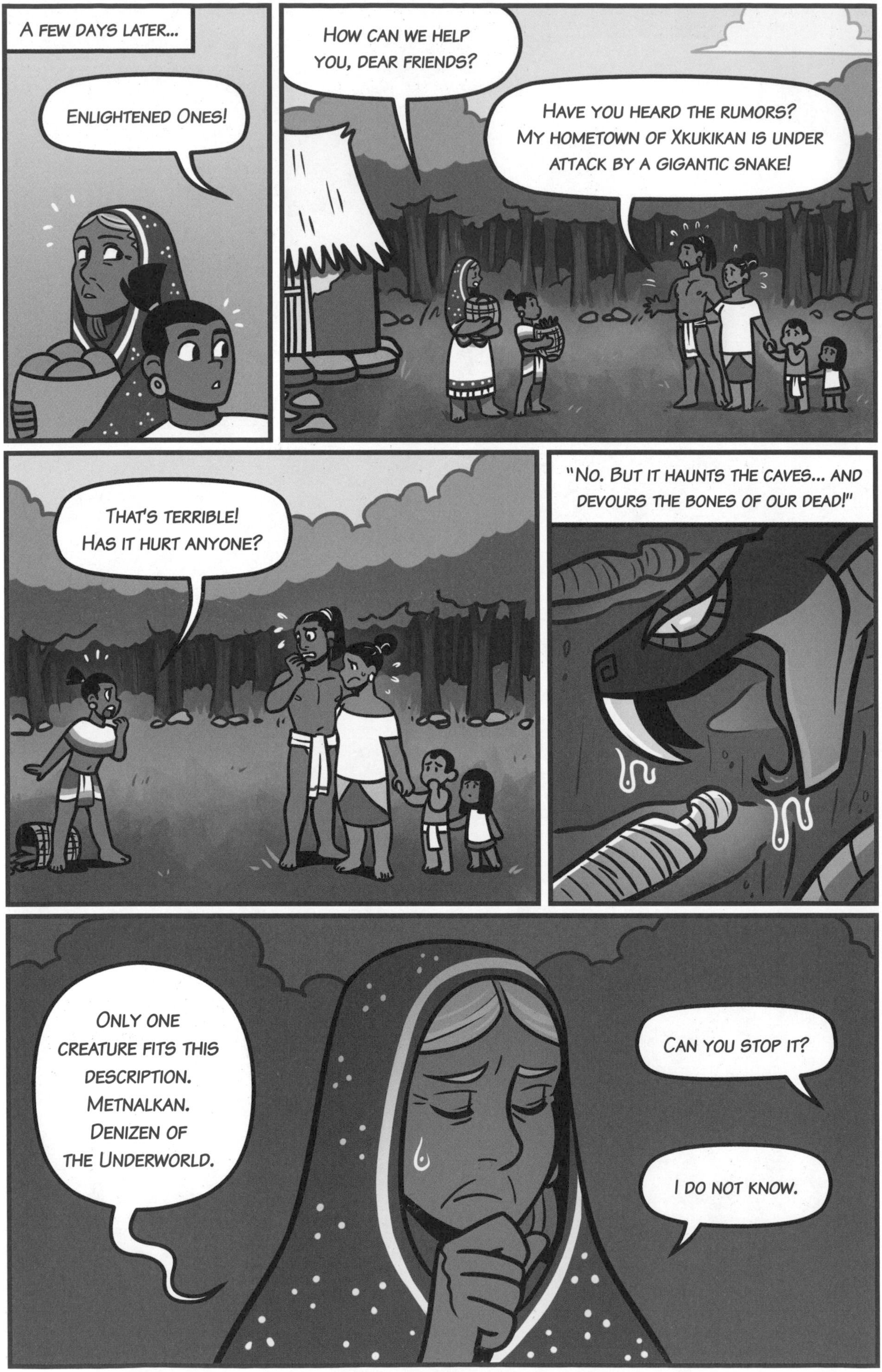
A FEW DAYS LATER...
ENLIGHTENED ONES!
HOW CAN WE HELP YOU, DEAR FRIENDS?
HAVE YOU HEARD THE RUMORS? MY HOMETOWN OF XKUKIKAN IS UNDER ATTACK BY A GIGANTIC SNAKE!
THAT'S TERRIBLE! HAS IT HURT ANYONE?
"NO. BUT IT HAUNTS THE CAVES... AND DEVOURS THE BONES OF OUR DEAD!"
ONLY ONE CREATURE FITS THIS DESCRIPTION. METNALKAN. DENIZEN OF THE UNDERWORLD.
CAN YOU STOP IT?
I DO NOT KNOW.

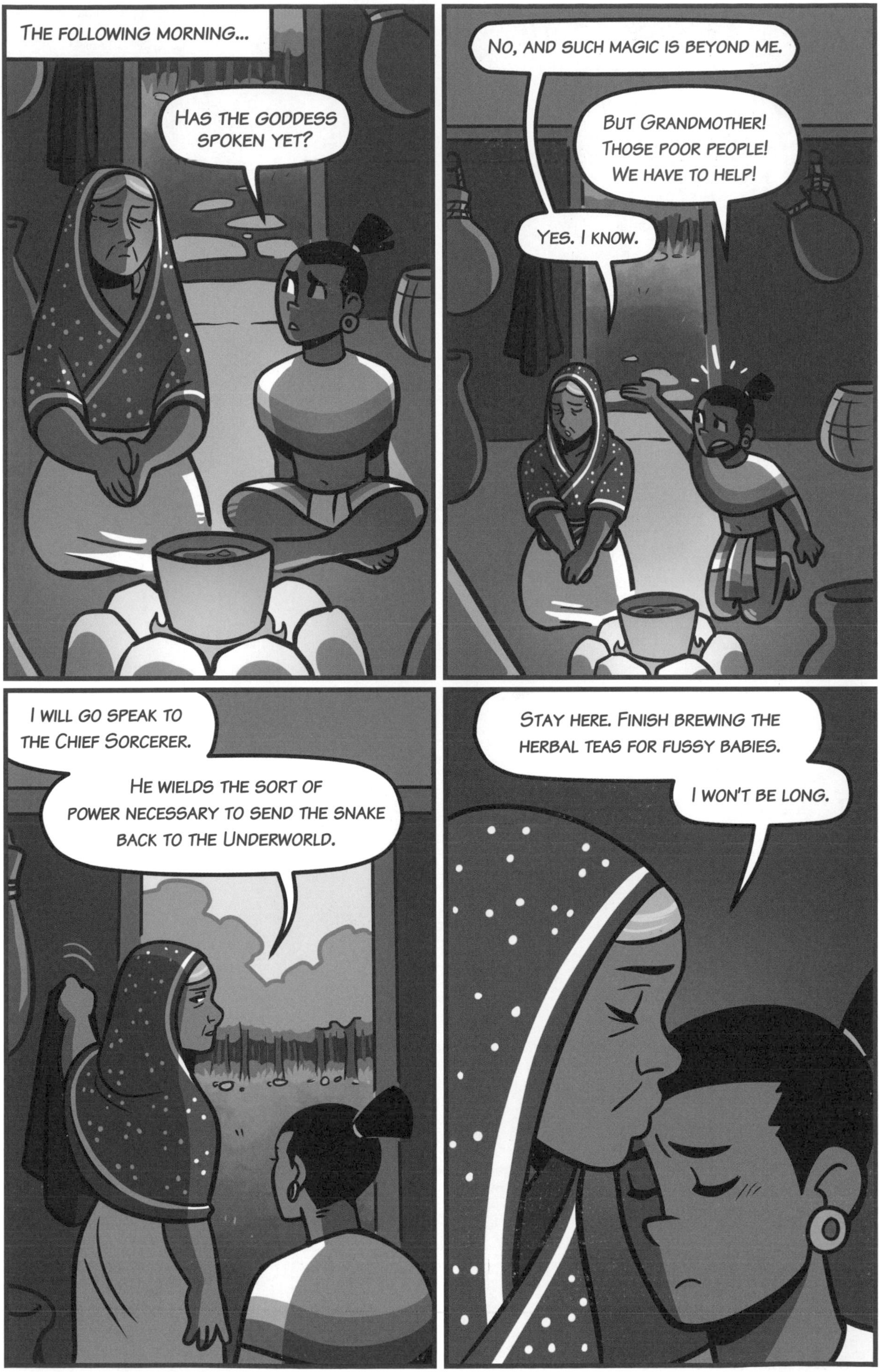
The following morning...
Has the goddess spoken yet?
No, and such magic is beyond me.
But Grandmother! Those poor people! We have to help!
Yes. I know.
I will go speak to the Chief Sorcerer.
He wields the sort of power necessary to send the snake back to the Underworld.
Stay here. Finish brewing the herbal teas for fussy babies.
I won't be long.

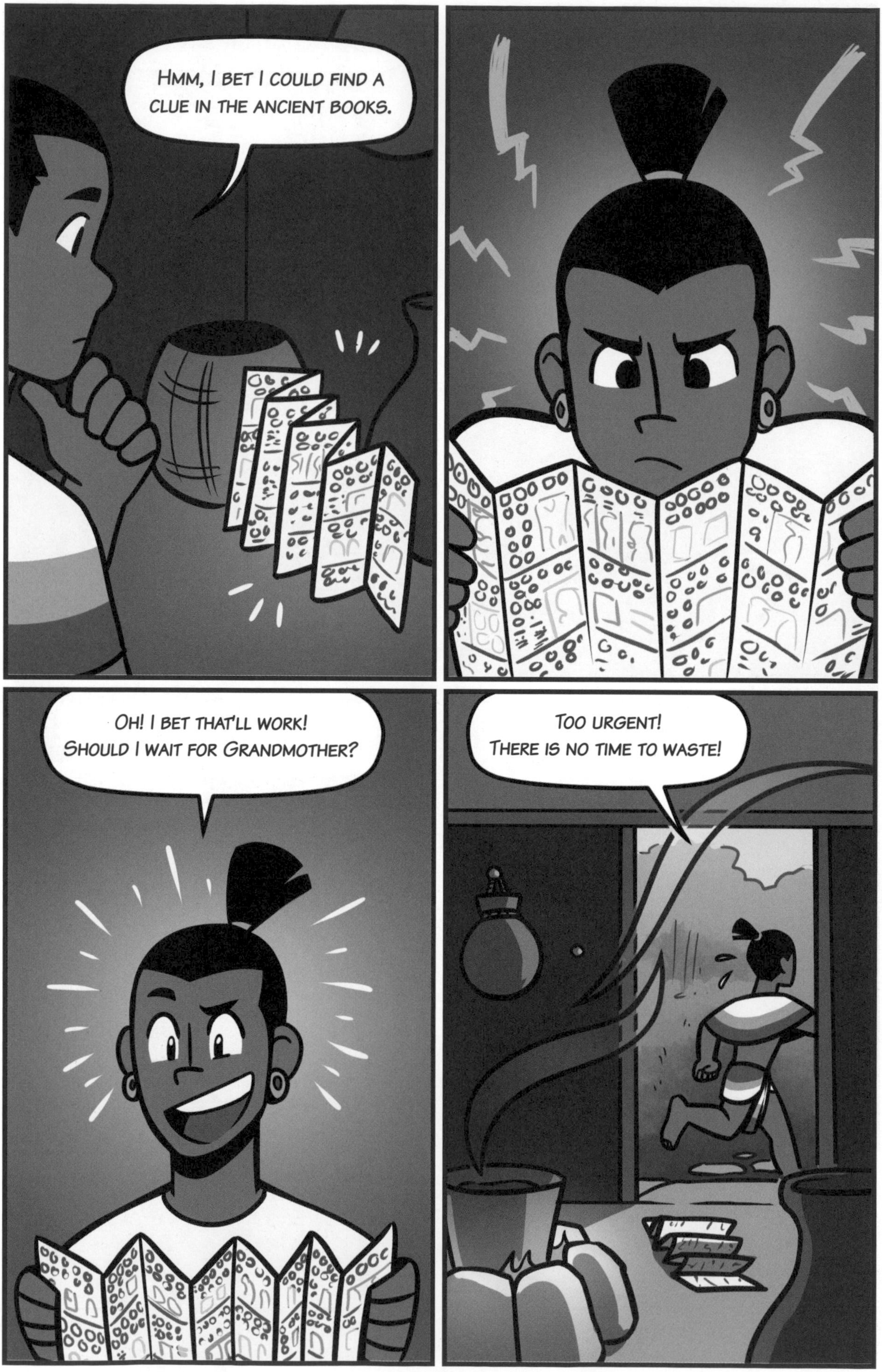
HMM, I BET I COULD FIND A CLUE IN THE ANCIENT BOOKS.
OH! I BET THAT'LL WORK! SHOULD I WAIT FOR GRANDMOTHER?
TOO URGENT! THERE IS NO TIME TO WASTE!

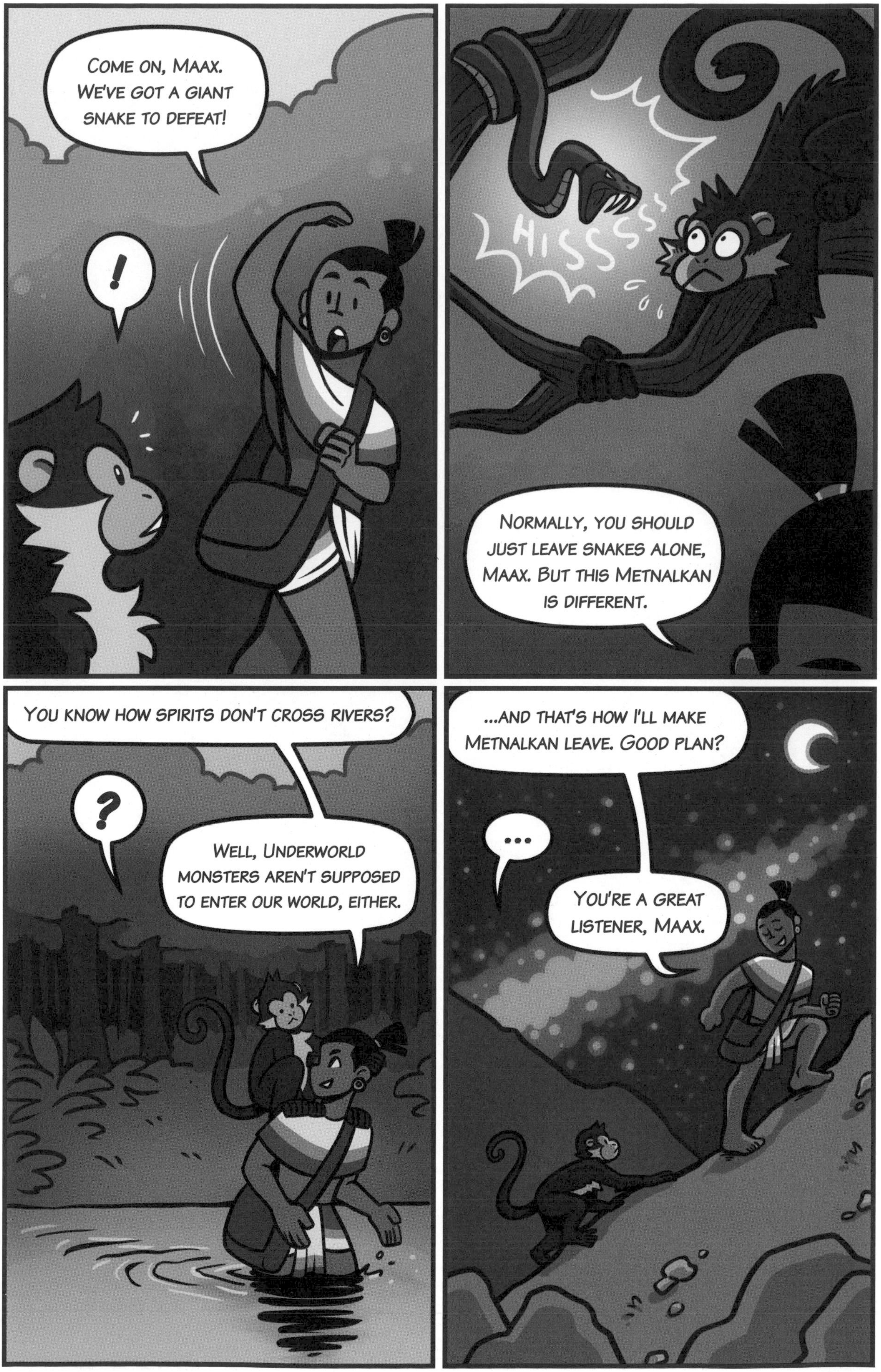
COME ON, MAAX. WE'VE GOT A GIANT SNAKE TO DEFEAT!
!
HISSSS
NORMALLY, YOU SHOULD JUST LEAVE SNAKES ALONE, MAAX. BUT THIS METNALKAN IS DIFFERENT.
YOU KNOW HOW SPIRITS DON'T CROSS RIVERS?
?
WELL, UNDERWORLD MONSTERS AREN'T SUPPOSED TO ENTER OUR WORLD, EITHER.
...AND THAT'S HOW I'LL MAKE METNALKAN LEAVE. GOOD PLAN?
...
YOU'RE A GREAT LISTENER, MAAX.

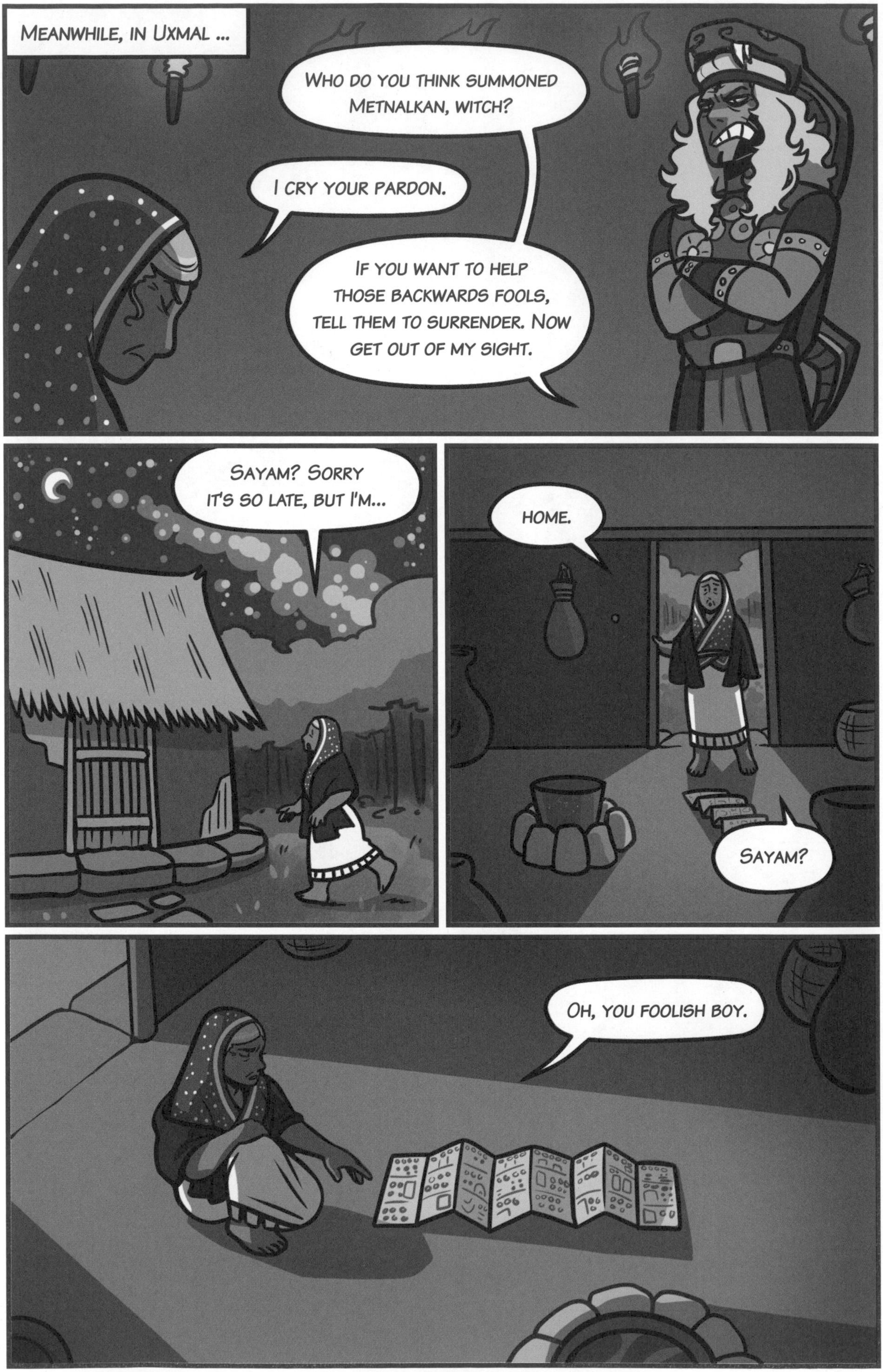

MEANWHILE, IN UXMAL ...
WHO DO YOU THINK SUMMONED METNALKAN, WITCH?
I CRY YOUR PARDON.
IF YOU WANT TO HELP THOSE BACKWARDS FOOLS, TELL THEM TO SURRENDER. NOW GET OUT OF MY SIGHT.
SAYAM? SORRY IT'S SO LATE, BUT I'M...
HOME.
SAYAM?
OH, YOU FOOLISH BOY.

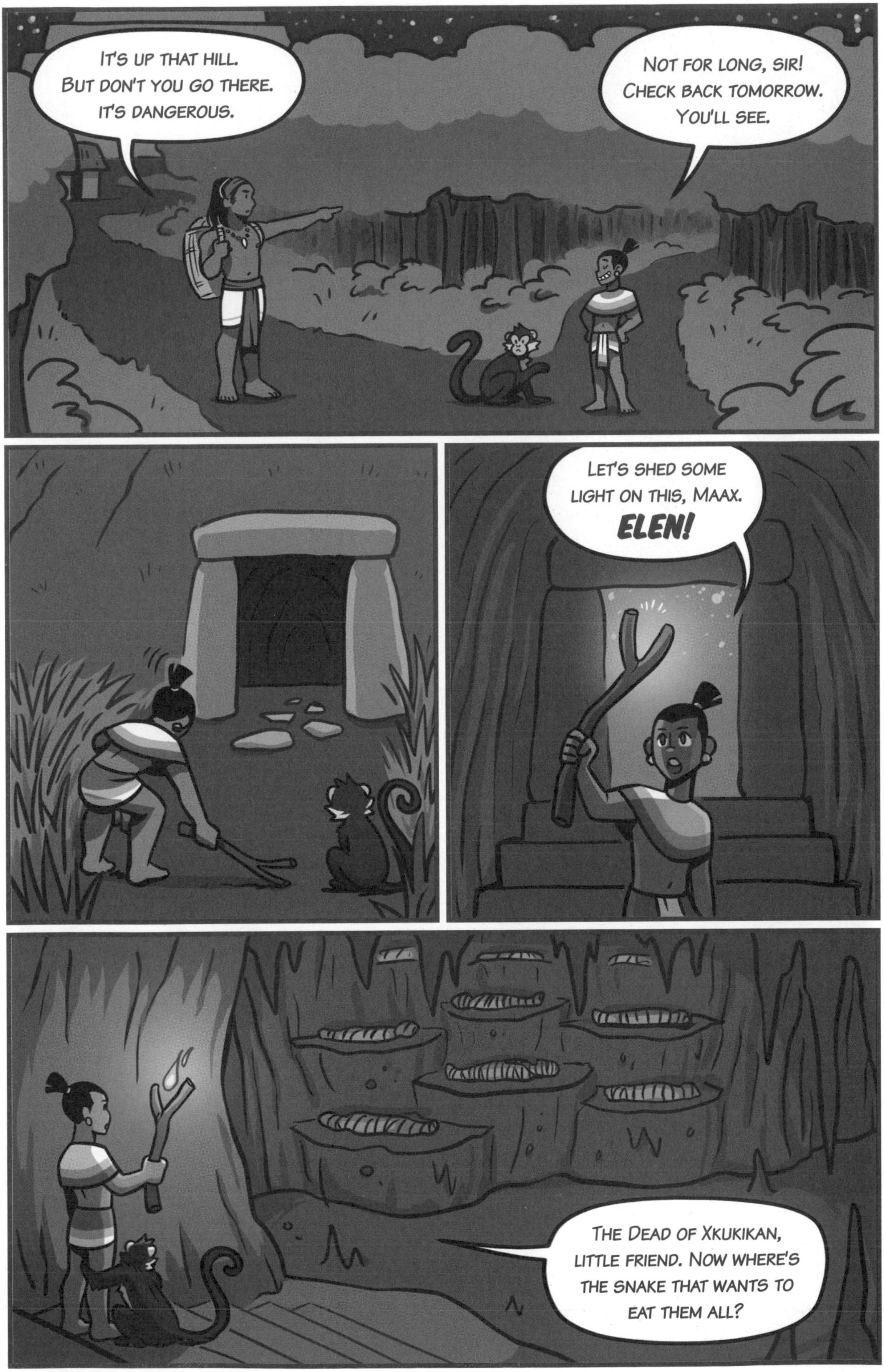
IT'S UP THAT HILL. BUT DON'T YOU GO THERE. IT'S DANGEROUS.
NOT FOR LONG, SIR! CHECK BACK TOMORROW. YOU'LL SEE.
LET'S SHED SOME LIGHT ON THIS, MAAX. ELEN!
THE DEAD OF XKUKIKAN, LITTLE FRIEND. NOW WHERE'S THE SNAKE THAT WANTS TO EAT THEM ALL?

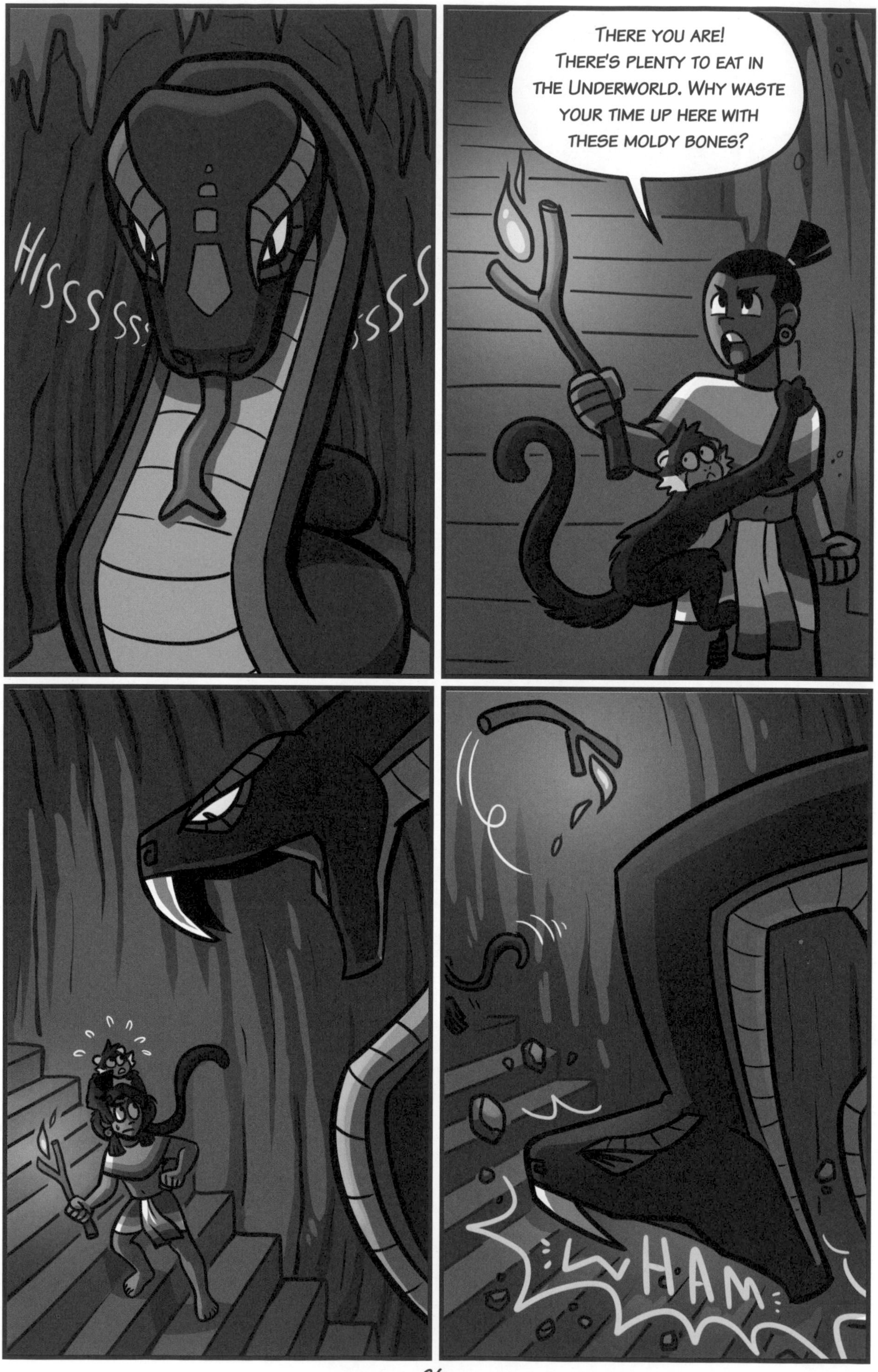
HISSSSSS
SSSS
THERE YOU ARE!
THERE'S PLENTY TO EAT IN THE UNDERWORLD. WHY WASTE YOUR TIME UP HERE WITH THESE MOLDY BONES?
WHAM

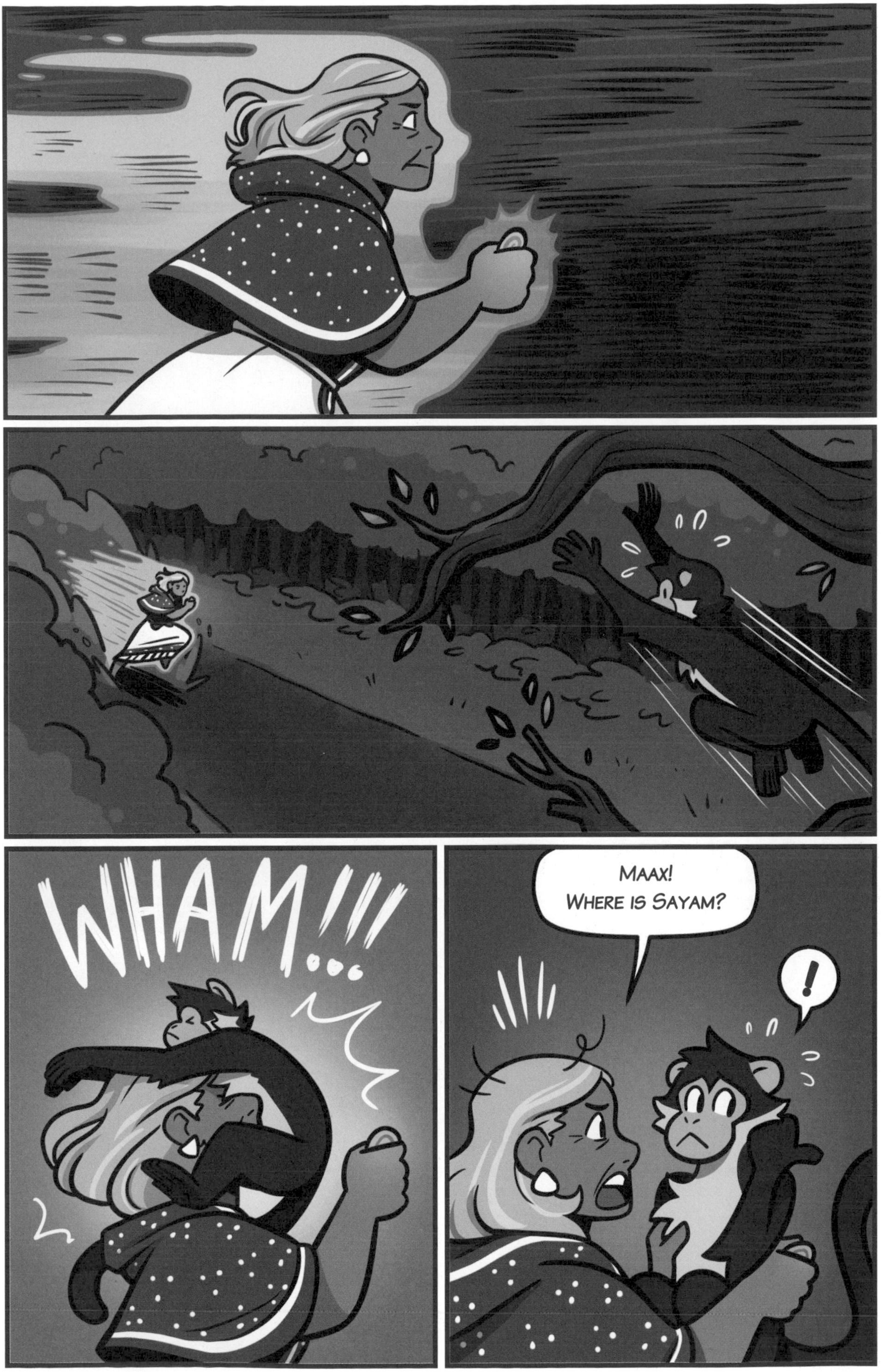
WHAM!!!
MAAX!
WHERE IS SAYAM?
!

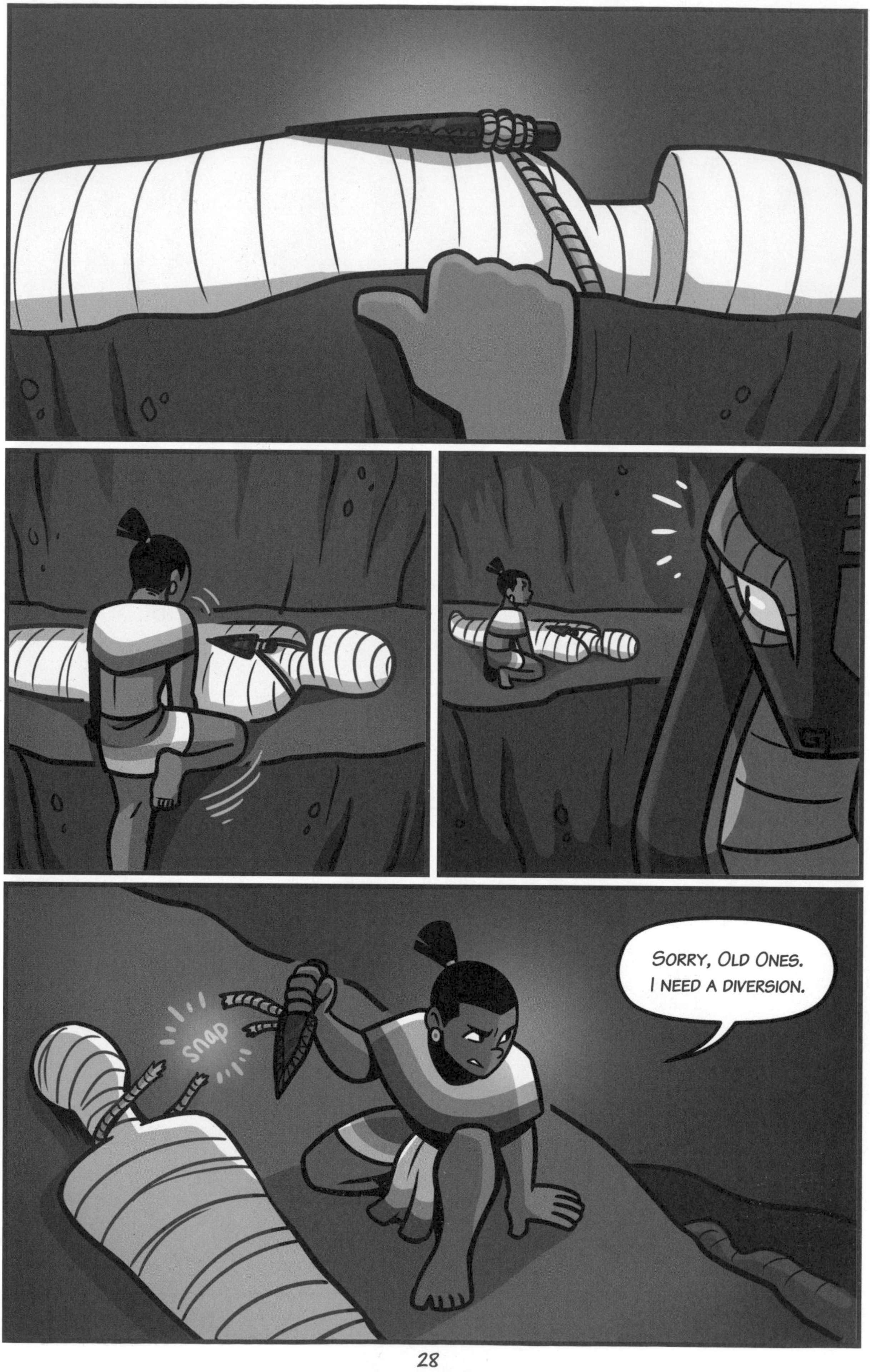
SORRY, OLD ONES.
I NEED A DIVERSION.
snap

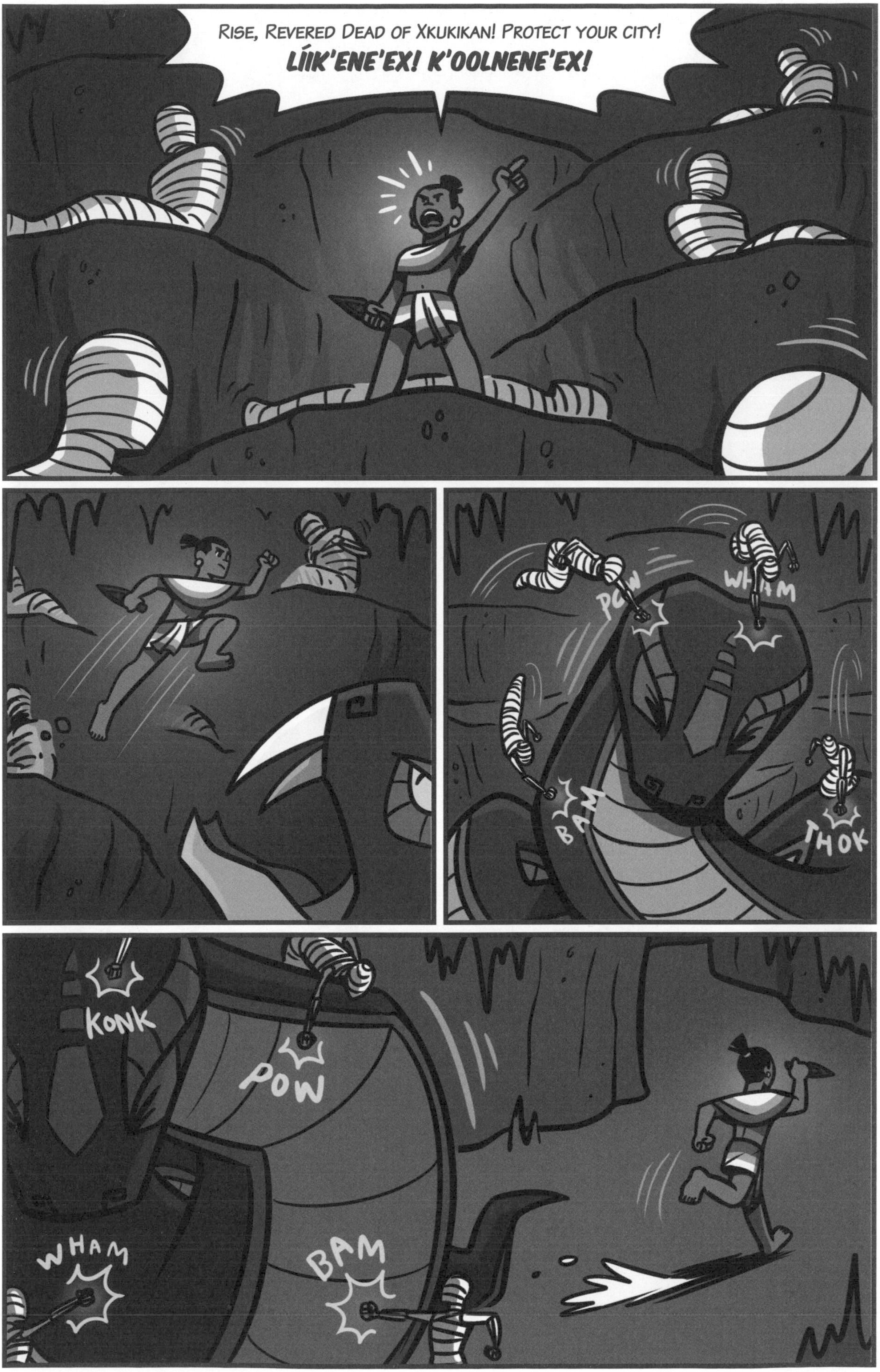

Rise, Revered Dead of Xkukikan! Protect your city!
LÍIK'ENE'EX! K'OOLNENE'EX!
POW
WHAM
BAM
THOK
KONK
POW
WHAM
BAM

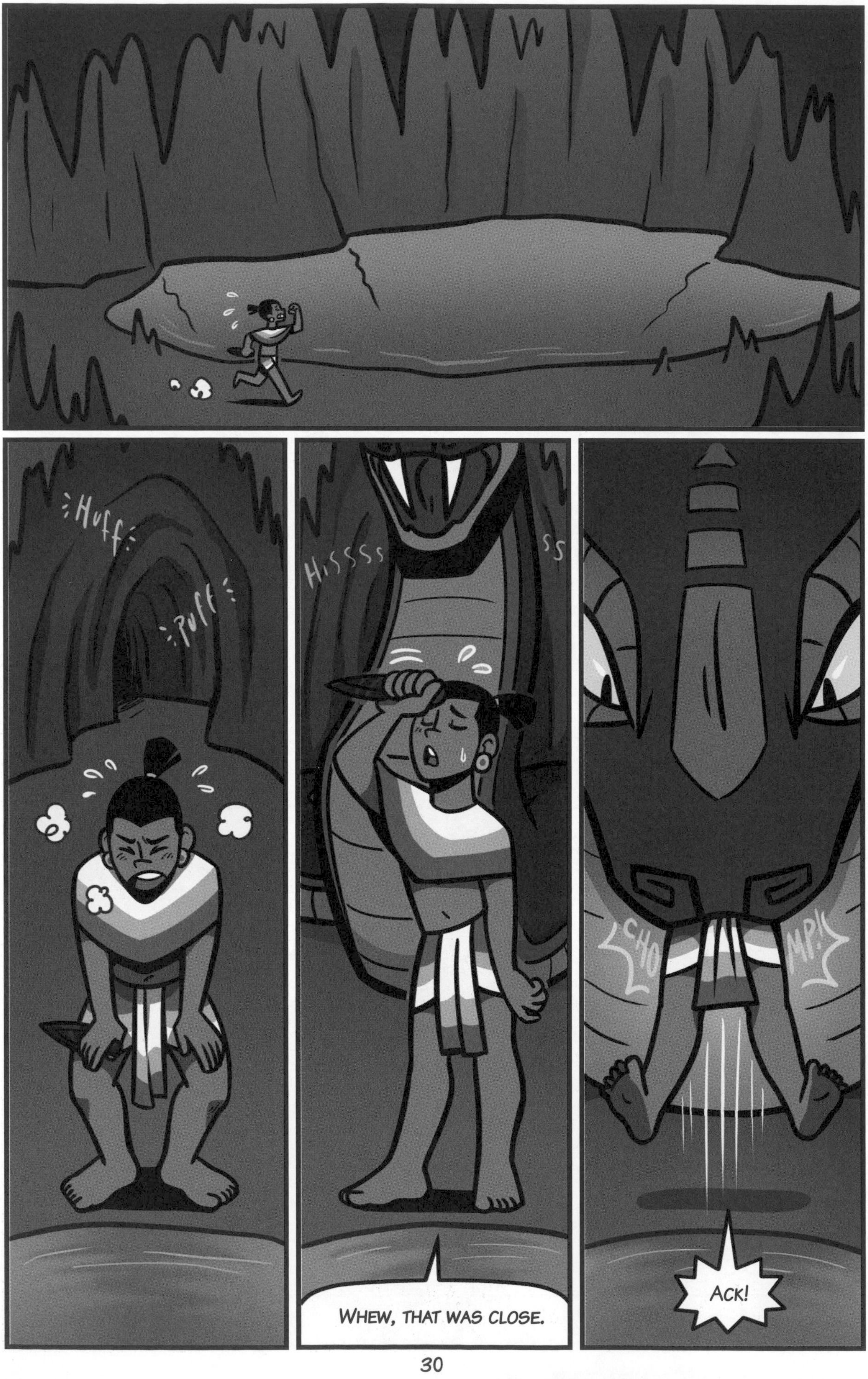
Huff
Puff
Hissss
ss
Whew, that was close.
CHOMP!
Ack!

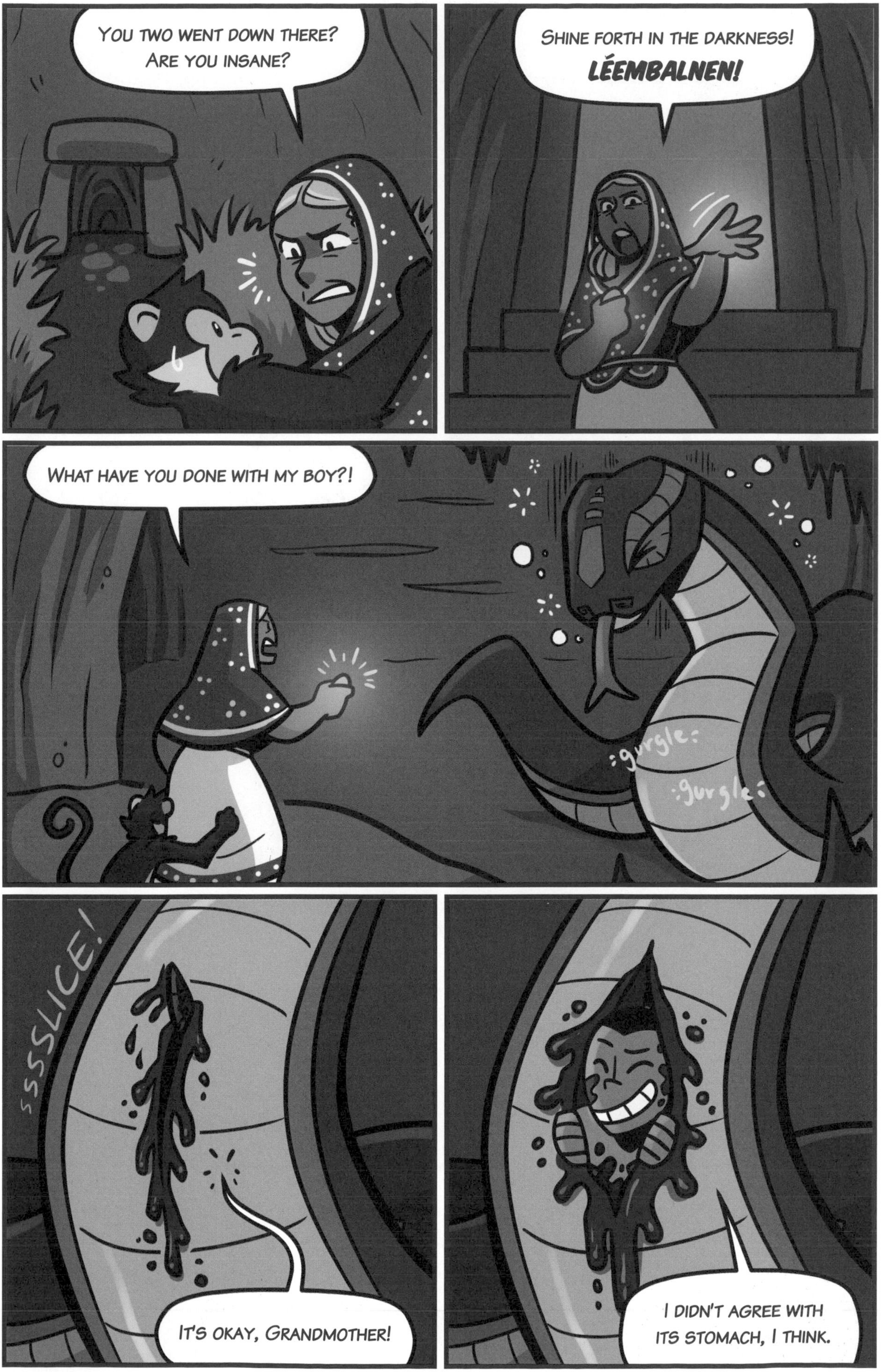

You two went down there? Are you insane?
Shine forth in the darkness! **Léembalnen!**
What have you done with my boy?!
:gurgle:
:gurgle:
sssSLICE!
It's okay, Grandmother!
I didn't agree with its stomach, I think.

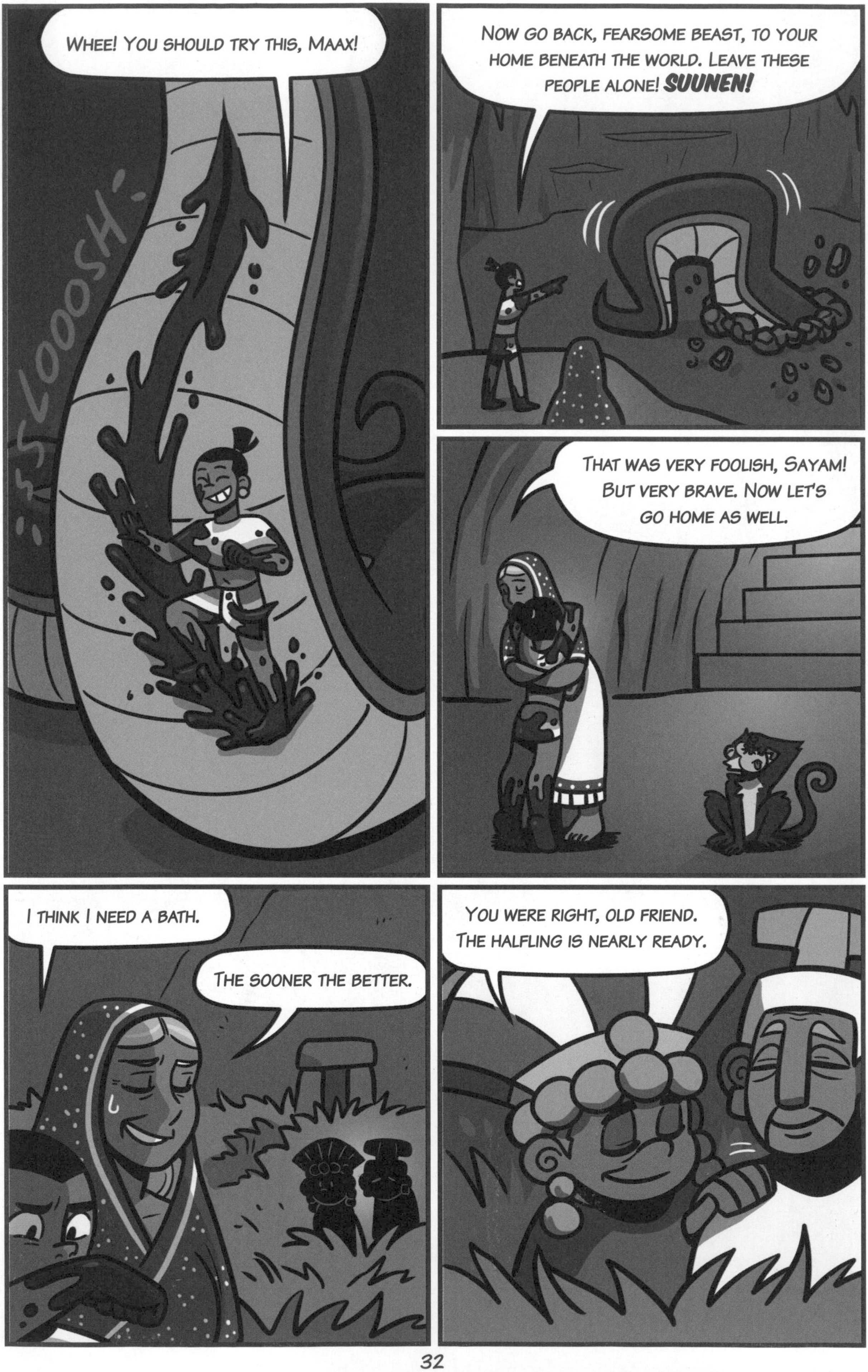
WHEE! YOU SHOULD TRY THIS, MAAX!
SSLOOOSH
NOW GO BACK, FEARSOME BEAST, TO YOUR HOME BENEATH THE WORLD. LEAVE THESE PEOPLE ALONE! SUUNEN!
THAT WAS VERY FOOLISH, SAYAM! BUT VERY BRAVE. NOW LET'S GO HOME AS WELL.
I THINK I NEED A BATH.
THE SOONER THE BETTER.
YOU WERE RIGHT, OLD FRIEND. THE HALFLING IS NEARLY READY.

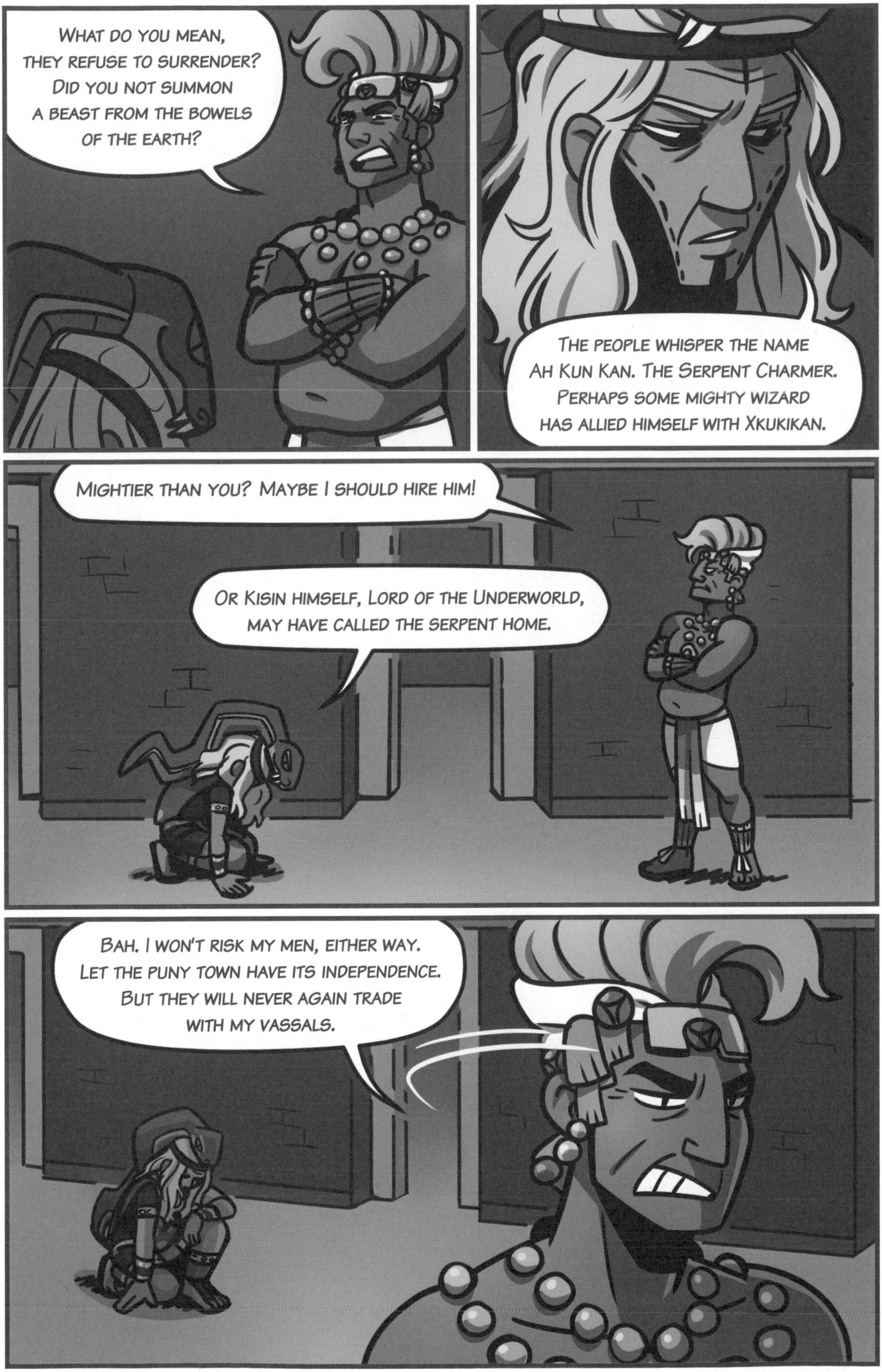
WHAT DO YOU MEAN, THEY REFUSE TO SURRENDER? DID YOU NOT SUMMON A BEAST FROM THE BOWELS OF THE EARTH?
THE PEOPLE WHISPER THE NAME AH KUN KAN. THE SERPENT CHARMER. PERHAPS SOME MIGHTY WIZARD HAS ALLIED HIMSELF WITH XKUKIKAN.
MIGHTIER THAN YOU? MAYBE I SHOULD HIRE HIM!
OR KISIN HIMSELF, LORD OF THE UNDERWORLD, MAY HAVE CALLED THE SERPENT HOME.
BAH. I WON'T RISK MY MEN, EITHER WAY. LET THE PUNY TOWN HAVE ITS INDEPENDENCE. BUT THEY WILL NEVER AGAIN TRADE WITH MY VASSALS.

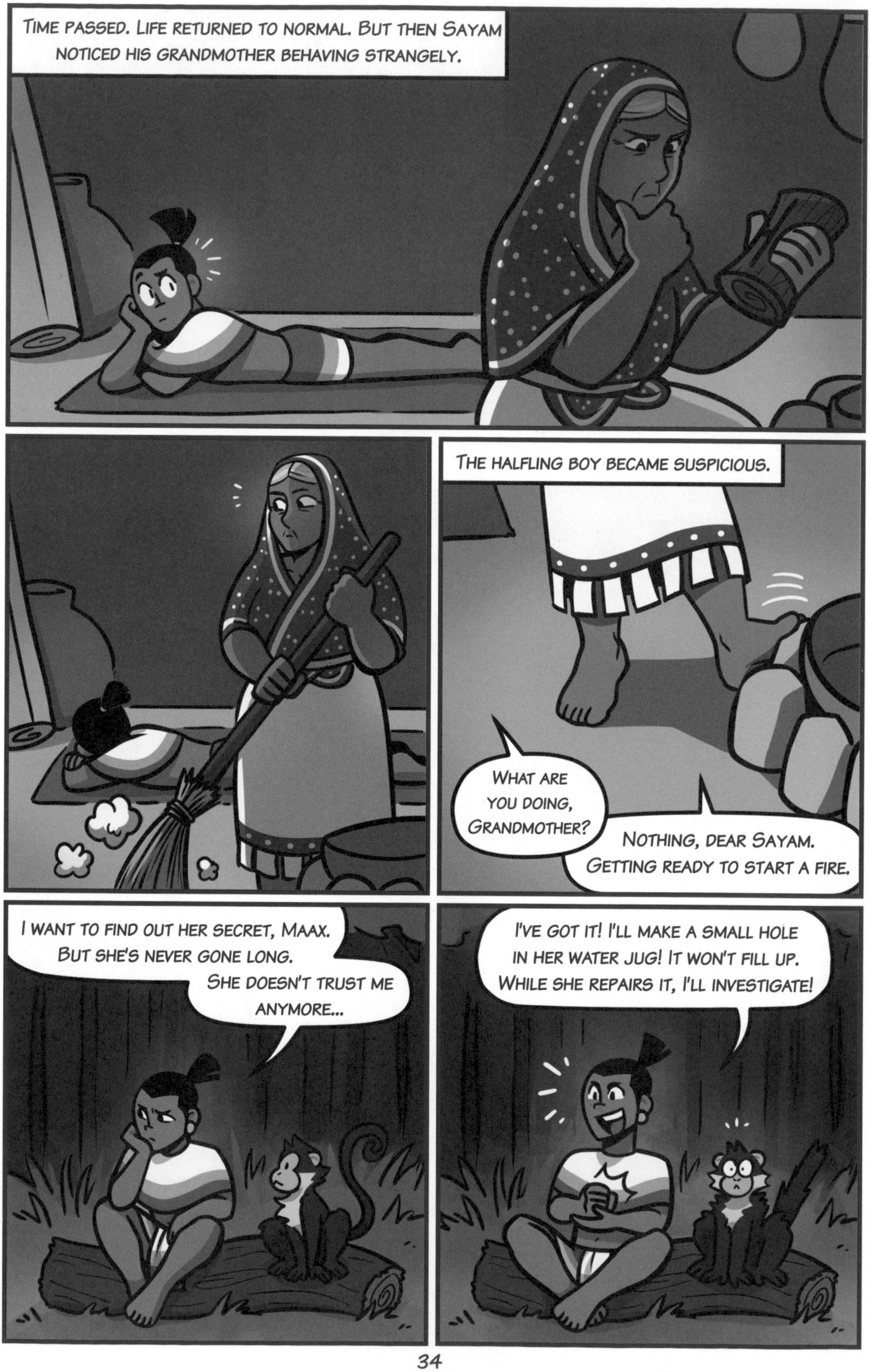
TIME PASSED. LIFE RETURNED TO NORMAL. BUT THEN SAYAM NOTICED HIS GRANDMOTHER BEHAVING STRANGELY.
THE HALFLING BOY BECAME SUSPICIOUS.
WHAT ARE YOU DOING, GRANDMOTHER?
NOTHING, DEAR SAYAM. GETTING READY TO START A FIRE.
I WANT TO FIND OUT HER SECRET, MAAX. BUT SHE'S NEVER GONE LONG.
SHE DOESN'T TRUST ME ANYMORE...
I'VE GOT IT! I'LL MAKE A SMALL HOLE IN HER WATER JUG! IT WON'T FILL UP. WHILE SHE REPAIRS IT, I'LL INVESTIGATE!

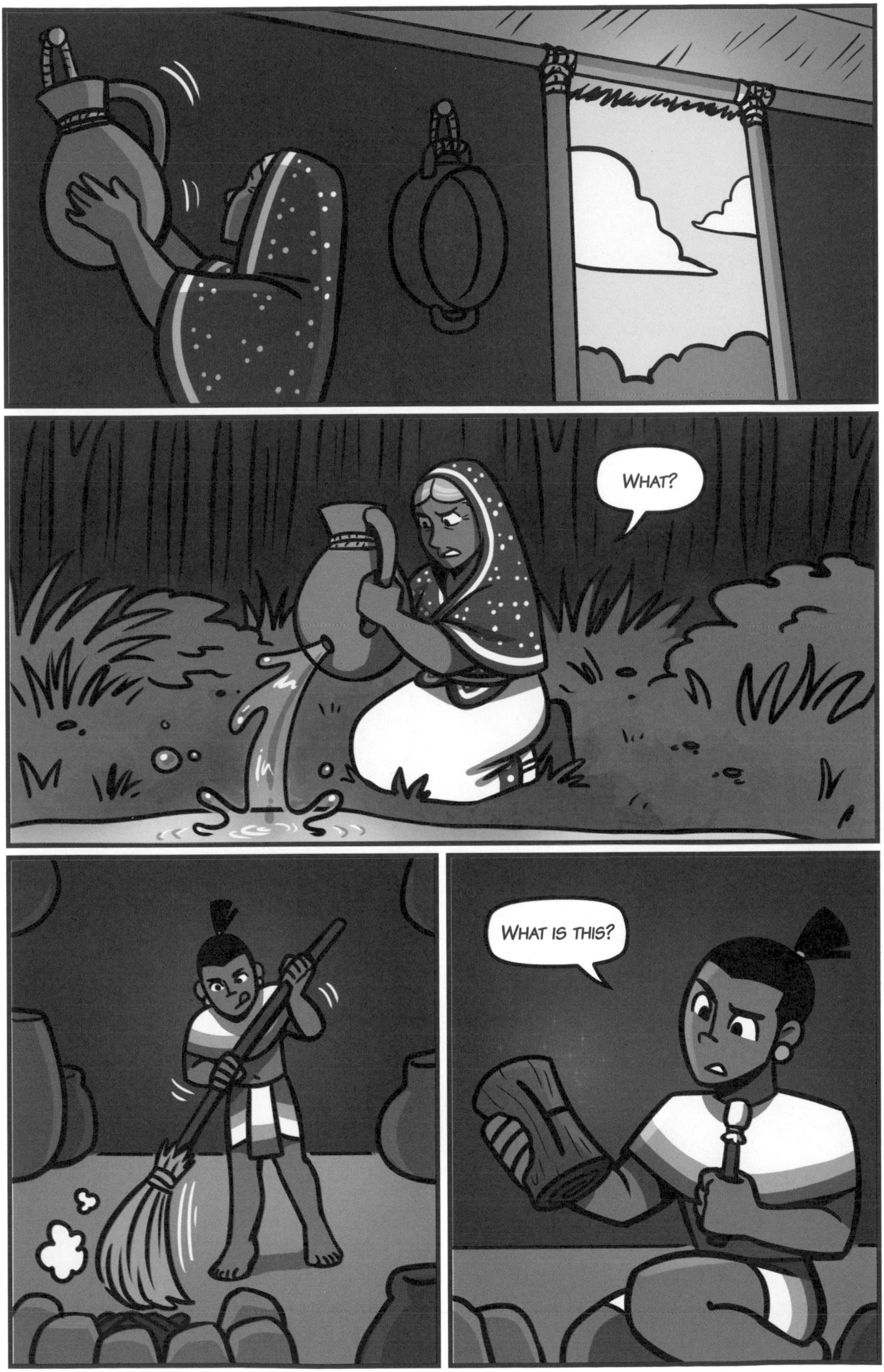
WHAT?
WHAT IS THIS?

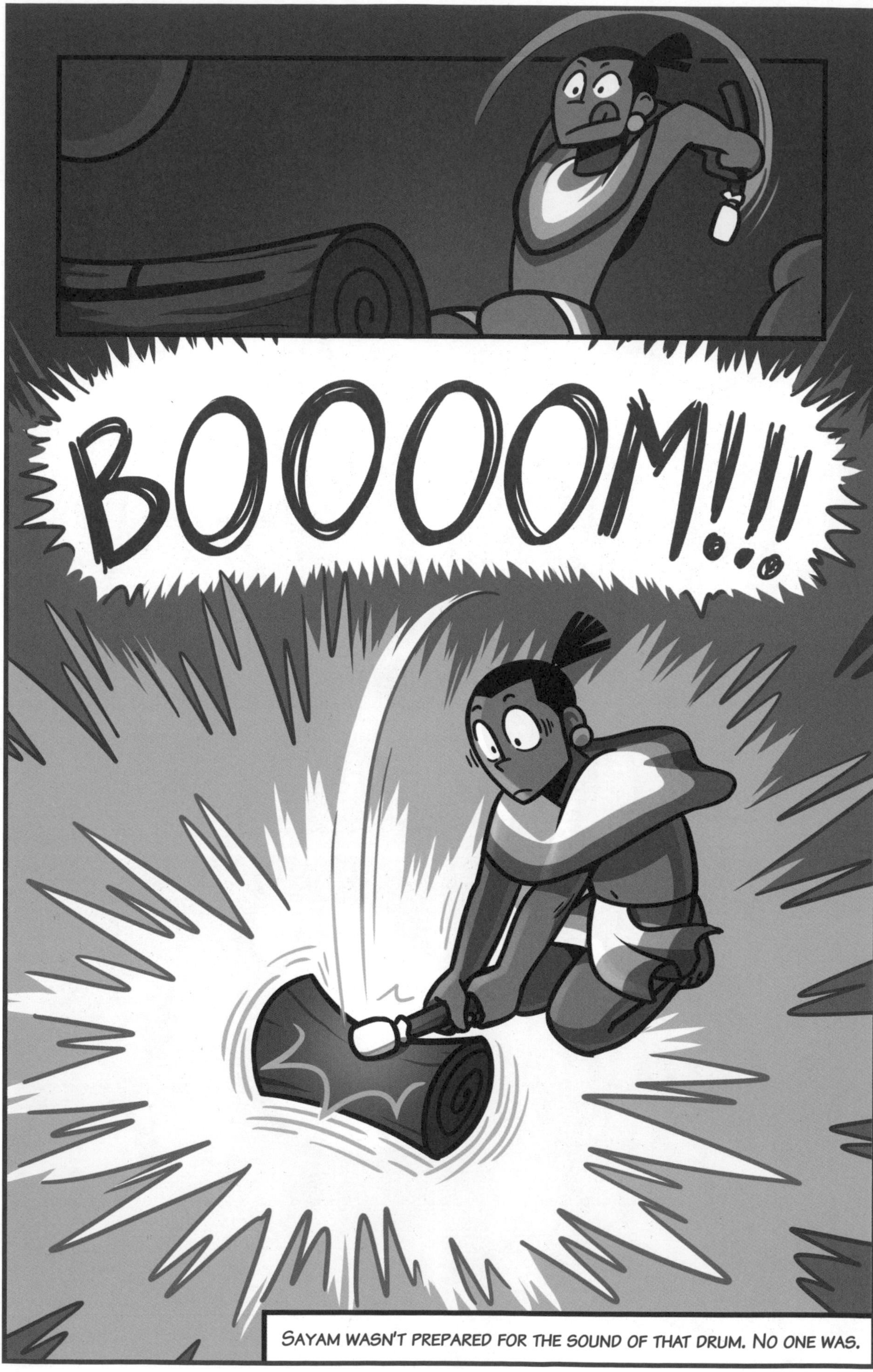
BOOOOM!!!
SAYAM WASN'T PREPARED FOR THE SOUND OF THAT DRUM. NO ONE WAS.

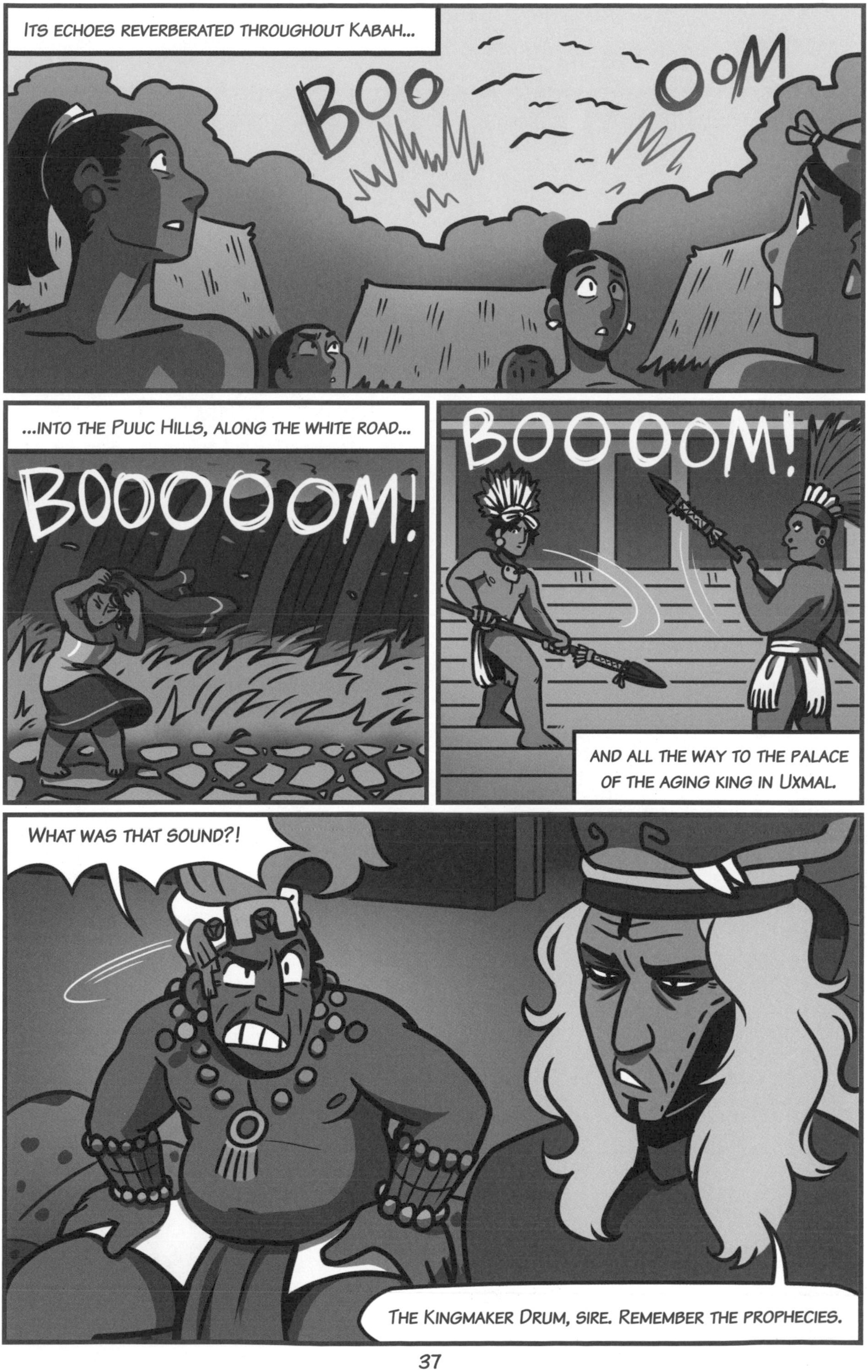

Its echoes reverberated throughout Kabah...
BOO
OOM
...into the Puuc Hills, along the white road...
BOOOOOM!
BOOOOM!
And all the way to the palace of the aging king in Uxmal.
What was that sound?!
The Kingmaker Drum, sire. Remember the prophecies.

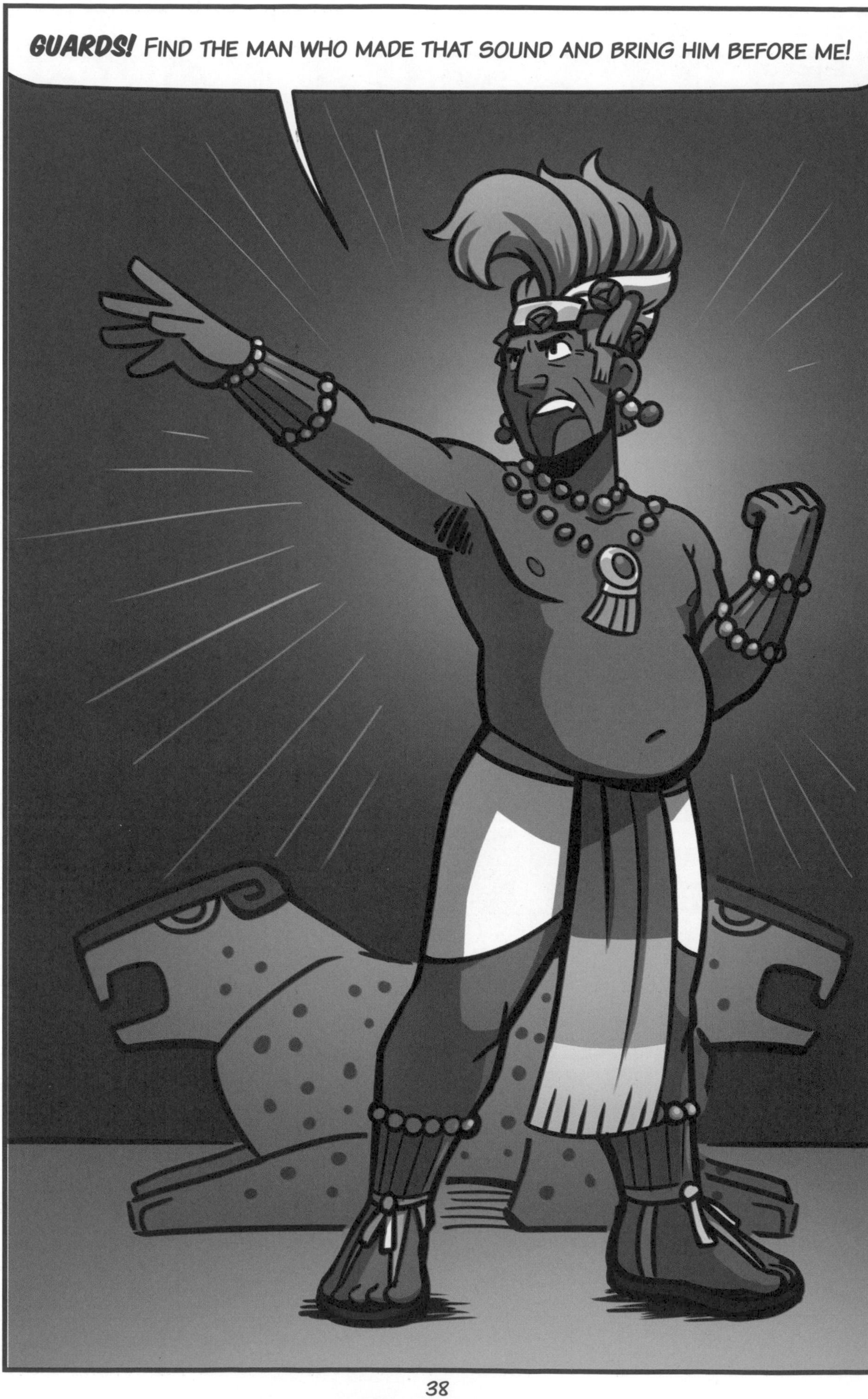
GUARDS! FIND THE MAN WHO MADE THAT SOUND AND BRING HIM BEFORE ME!

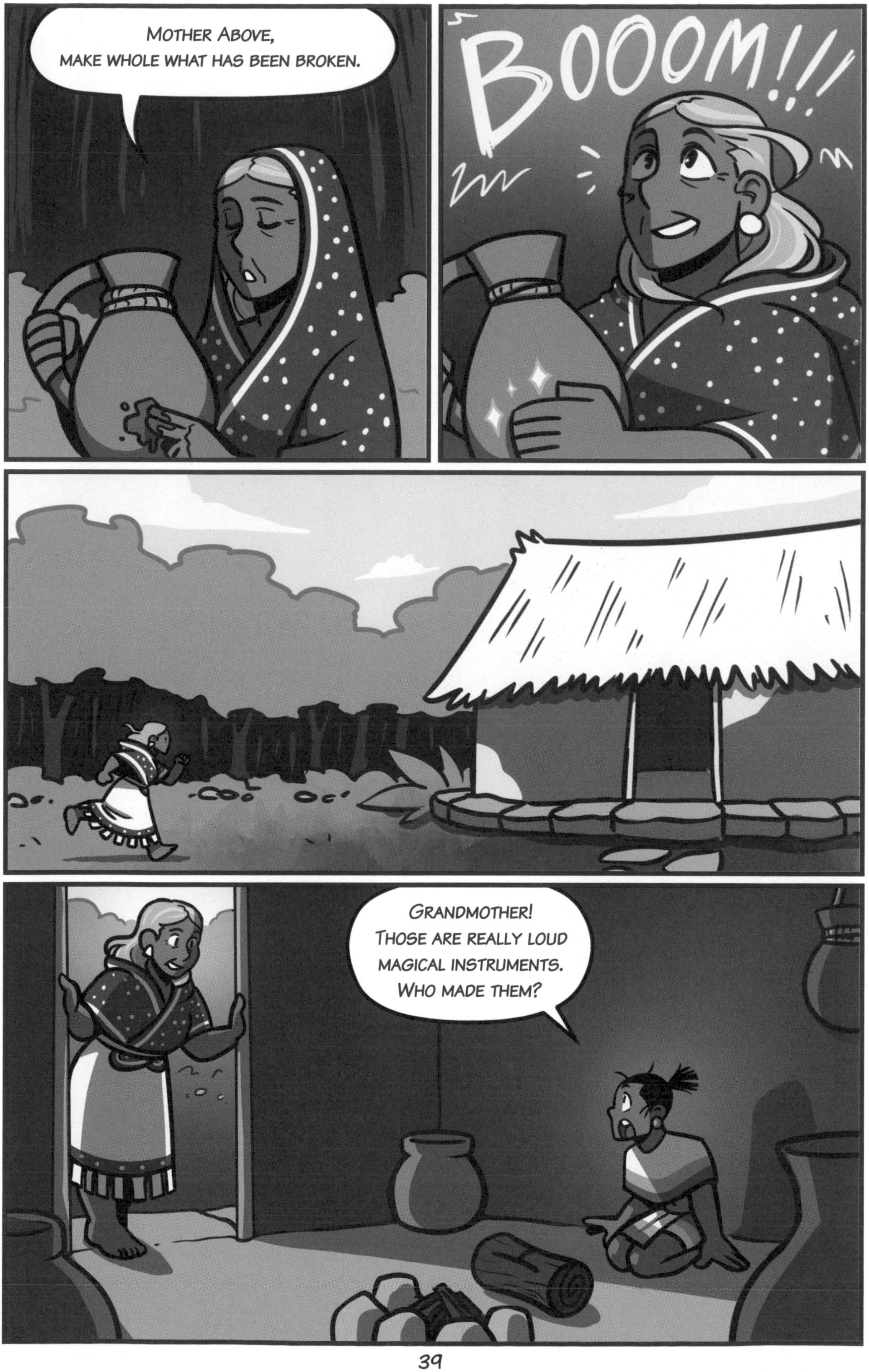
MOTHER ABOVE,
MAKE WHOLE WHAT HAS BEEN BROKEN.
BOOOM!!!
GRANDMOTHER!
THOSE ARE REALLY LOUD
MAGICAL INSTRUMENTS.
WHO MADE THEM?

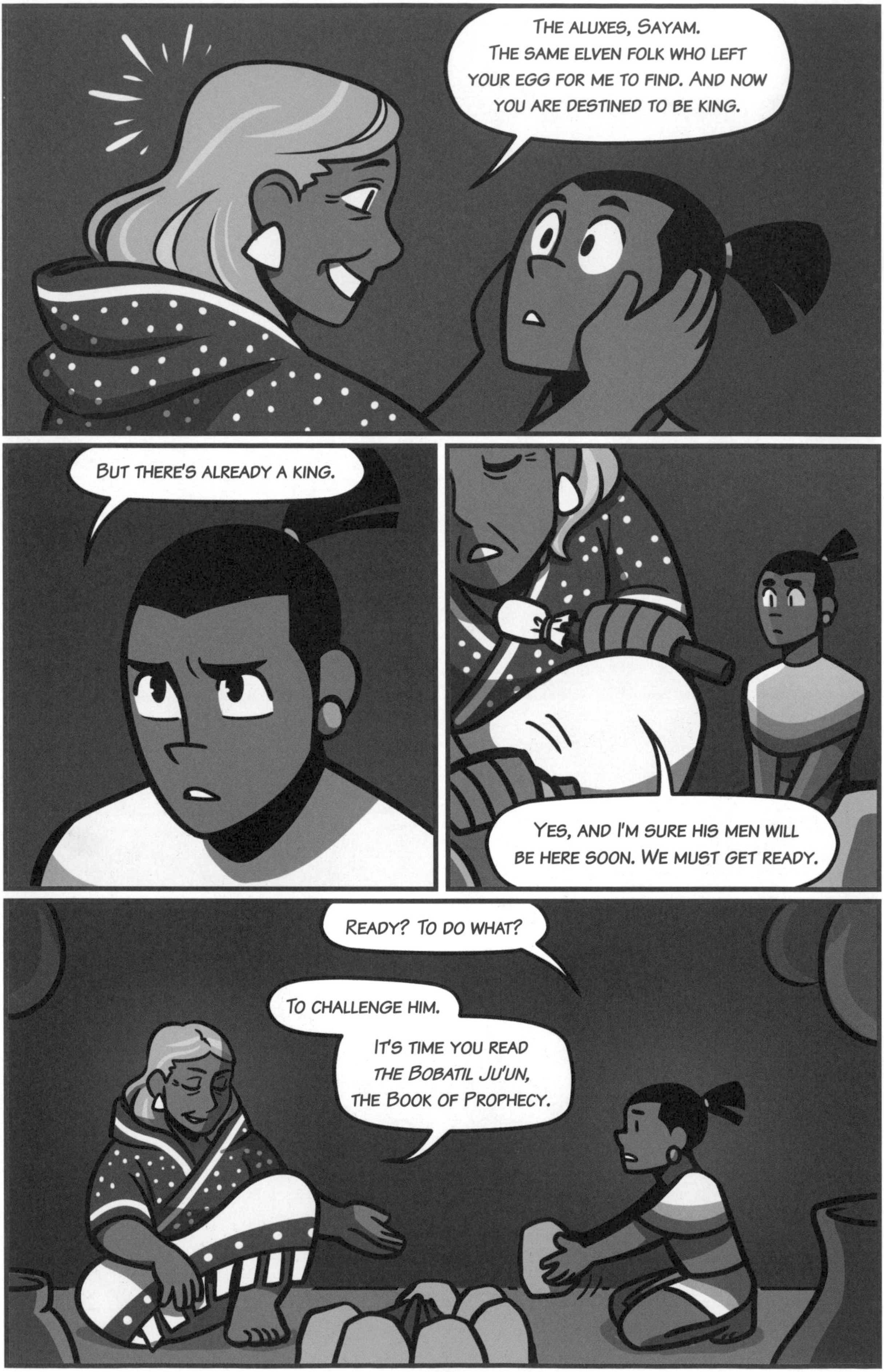
THE ALUXES, SAYAM. THE SAME ELVEN FOLK WHO LEFT YOUR EGG FOR ME TO FIND. AND NOW YOU ARE DESTINED TO BE KING.
BUT THERE'S ALREADY A KING.
YES, AND I'M SURE HIS MEN WILL BE HERE SOON. WE MUST GET READY.
READY? TO DO WHAT?
TO CHALLENGE HIM.
IT'S TIME YOU READ *THE BOBATIL JU'UN*, THE BOOK OF PROPHECY.

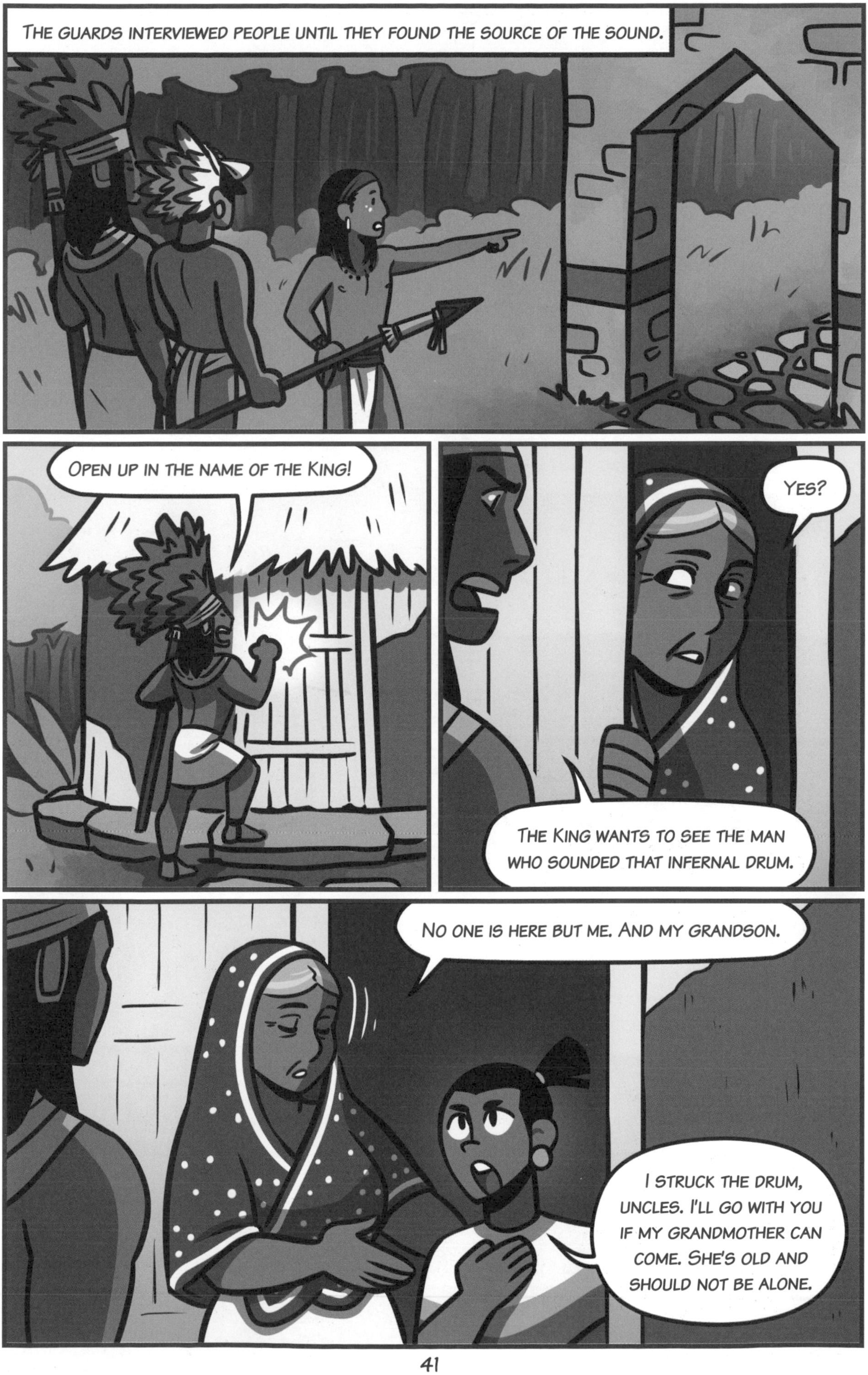
THE GUARDS INTERVIEWED PEOPLE UNTIL THEY FOUND THE SOURCE OF THE SOUND.
OPEN UP IN THE NAME OF THE KING!
YES?
THE KING WANTS TO SEE THE MAN WHO SOUNDED THAT INFERNAL DRUM.
NO ONE IS HERE BUT ME. AND MY GRANDSON.
I STRUCK THE DRUM, UNCLES. I'LL GO WITH YOU IF MY GRANDMOTHER CAN COME. SHE'S OLD AND SHOULD NOT BE ALONE.

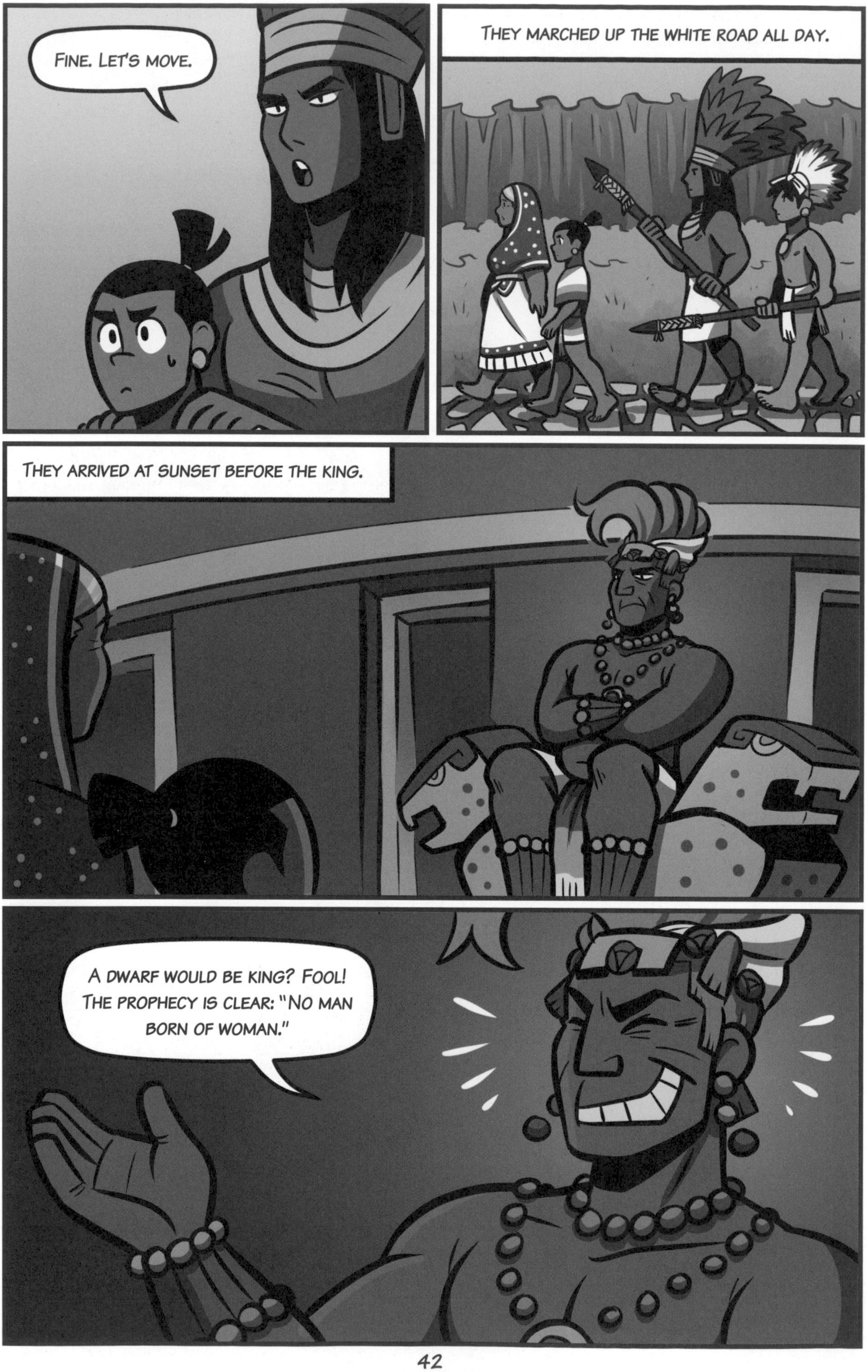
FINE. LET'S MOVE.
THEY MARCHED UP THE WHITE ROAD ALL DAY.
THEY ARRIVED AT SUNSET BEFORE THE KING.
A DWARF WOULD BE KING? FOOL! THE PROPHECY IS CLEAR: "NO MAN BORN OF WOMAN."

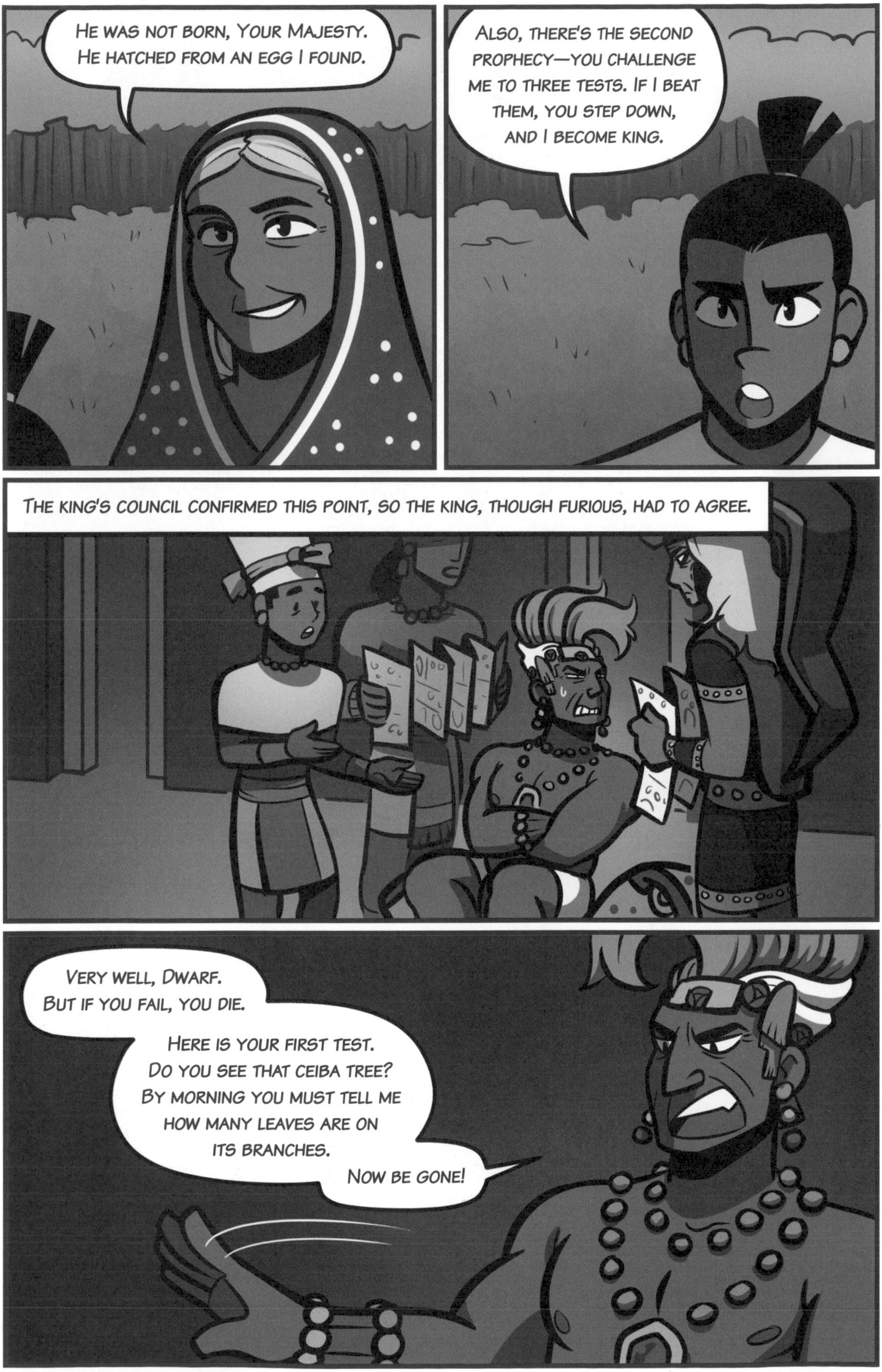
HE WAS NOT BORN, YOUR MAJESTY. HE HATCHED FROM AN EGG I FOUND.
ALSO, THERE'S THE SECOND PROPHECY—YOU CHALLENGE ME TO THREE TESTS. IF I BEAT THEM, YOU STEP DOWN, AND I BECOME KING.
THE KING'S COUNCIL CONFIRMED THIS POINT, SO THE KING, THOUGH FURIOUS, HAD TO AGREE.
VERY WELL, DWARF. BUT IF YOU FAIL, YOU DIE.
HERE IS YOUR FIRST TEST. DO YOU SEE THAT CEIBA TREE? BY MORNING YOU MUST TELL ME HOW MANY LEAVES ARE ON ITS BRANCHES.
NOW BE GONE!

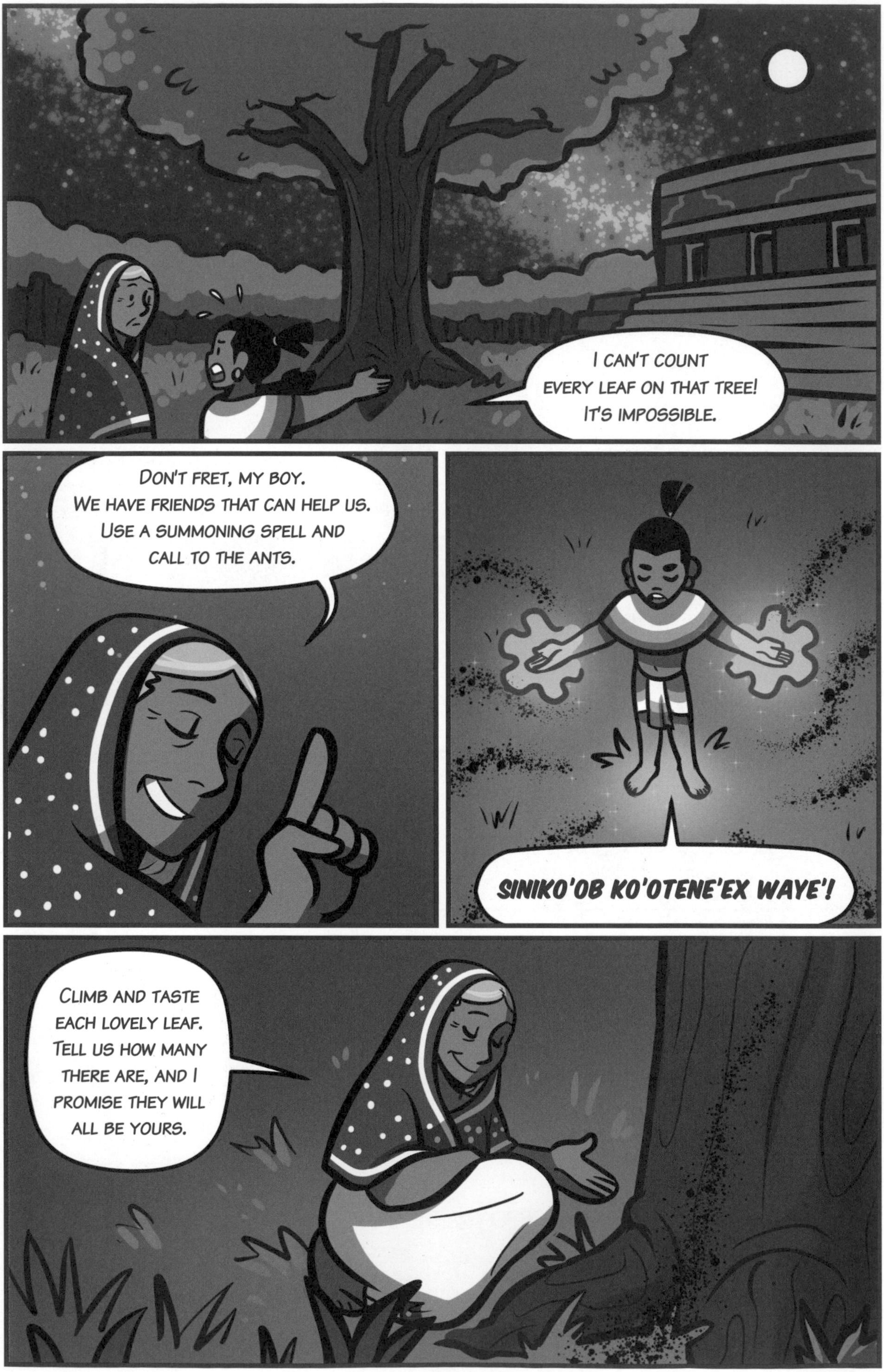
I CAN'T COUNT EVERY LEAF ON THAT TREE! IT'S IMPOSSIBLE.
DON'T FRET, MY BOY. WE HAVE FRIENDS THAT CAN HELP US. USE A SUMMONING SPELL AND CALL TO THE ANTS.
SINIKO'OB KO'OTENE'EX WAYE'!
CLIMB AND TASTE EACH LOVELY LEAF. TELL US HOW MANY THERE ARE, AND I PROMISE THEY WILL ALL BE YOURS.

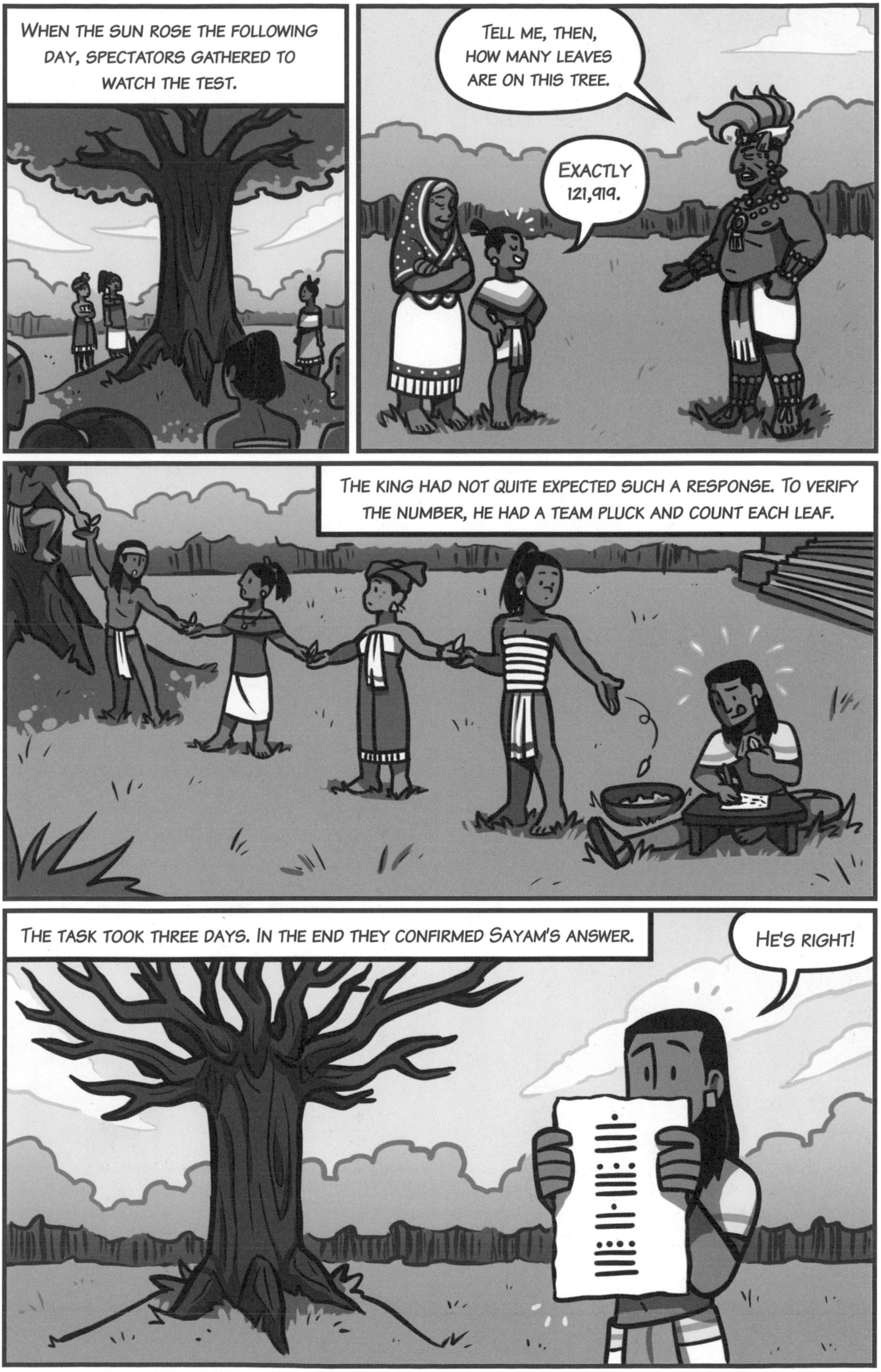

WHEN THE SUN ROSE THE FOLLOWING DAY, SPECTATORS GATHERED TO WATCH THE TEST.
TELL ME, THEN, HOW MANY LEAVES ARE ON THIS TREE.
EXACTLY 121,919.
THE KING HAD NOT QUITE EXPECTED SUCH A RESPONSE. TO VERIFY THE NUMBER, HE HAD A TEAM PLUCK AND COUNT EACH LEAF.
THE TASK TOOK THREE DAYS. IN THE END THEY CONFIRMED SAYAM'S ANSWER.
HE'S RIGHT!

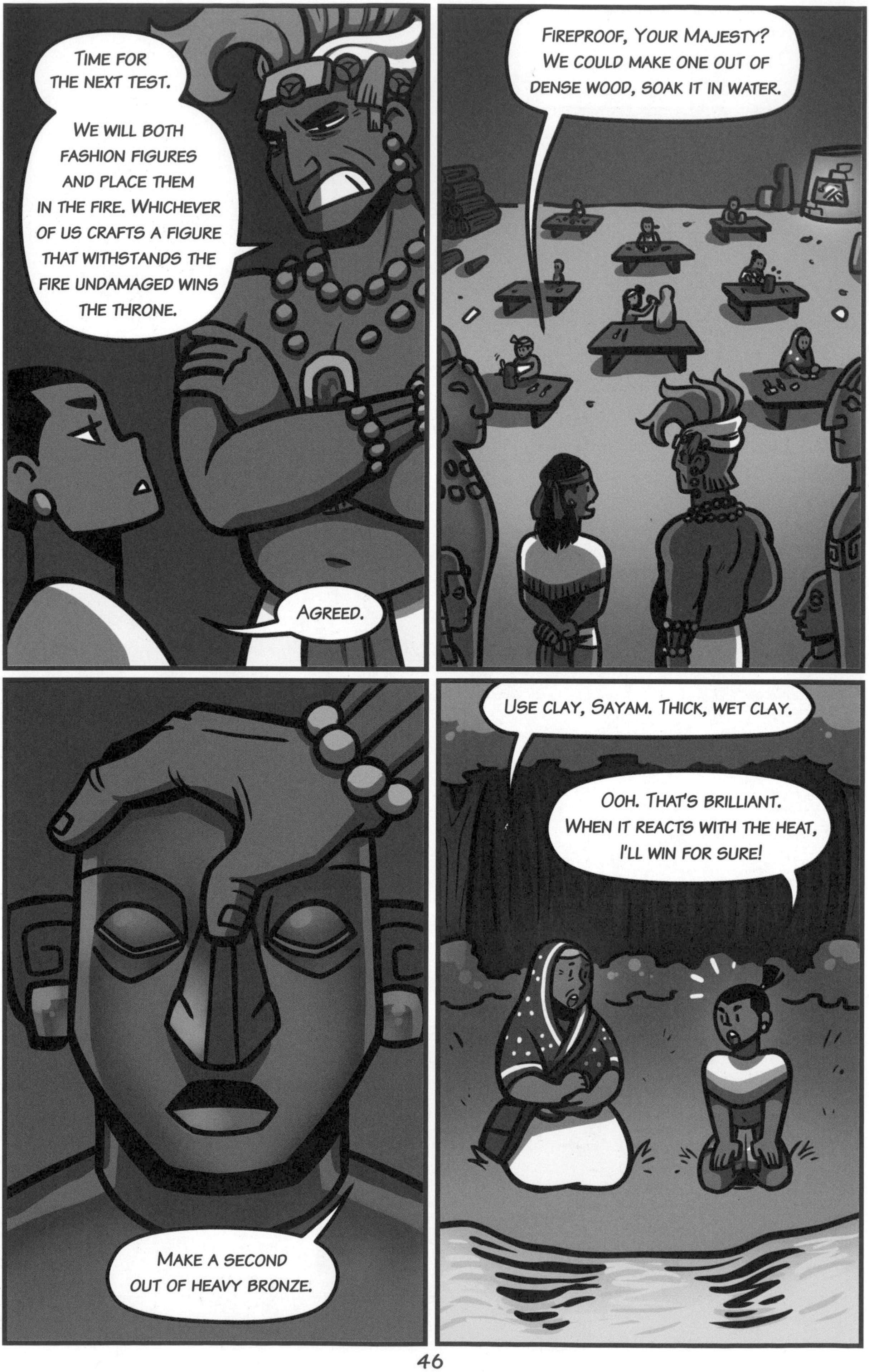
Time for the next test.
We will both fashion figures and place them in the fire. Whichever of us crafts a figure that withstands the fire undamaged wins the throne.
Agreed.
Fireproof, Your Majesty? We could make one out of dense wood, soak it in water.
Make a second out of heavy bronze.
Use clay, Sayam. Thick, wet clay.
Ooh. That's brilliant. When it reacts with the heat, I'll win for sure!

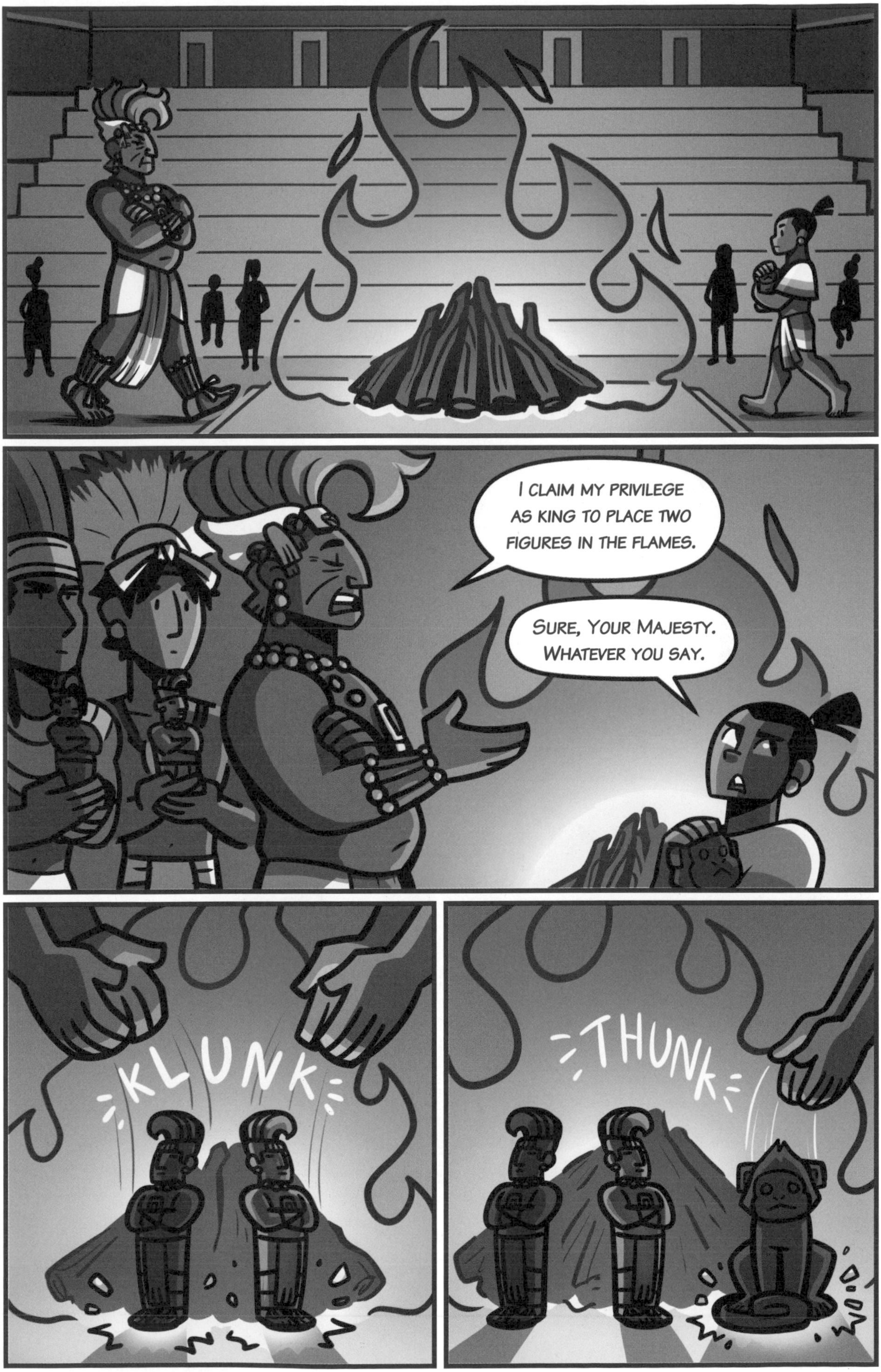
I CLAIM MY PRIVILEGE AS KING TO PLACE TWO FIGURES IN THE FLAMES.
SURE, YOUR MAJESTY. WHATEVER YOU SAY.
KLUNK
THUNK

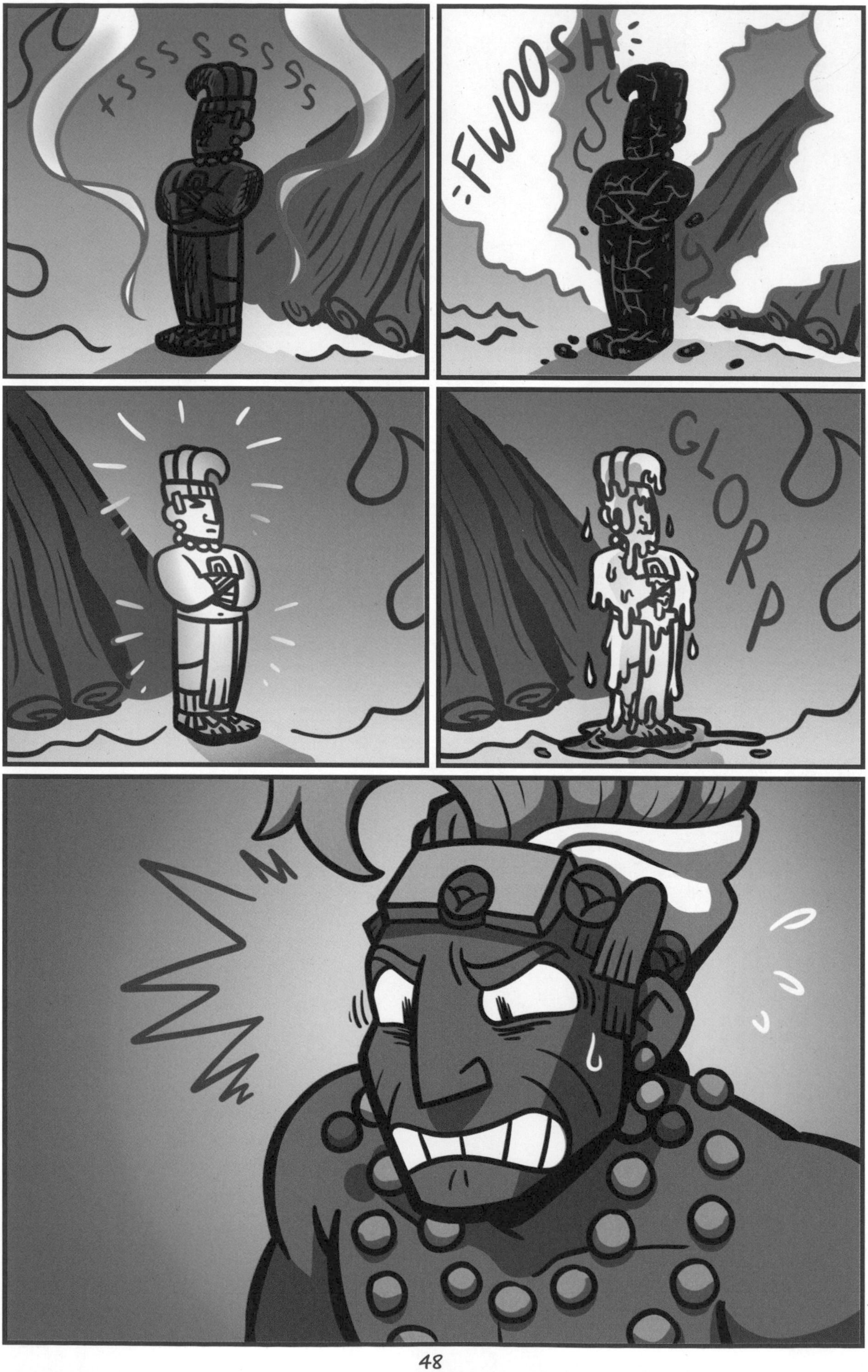
TSSSSSSSS
FWOOSH
GLORP
MMM

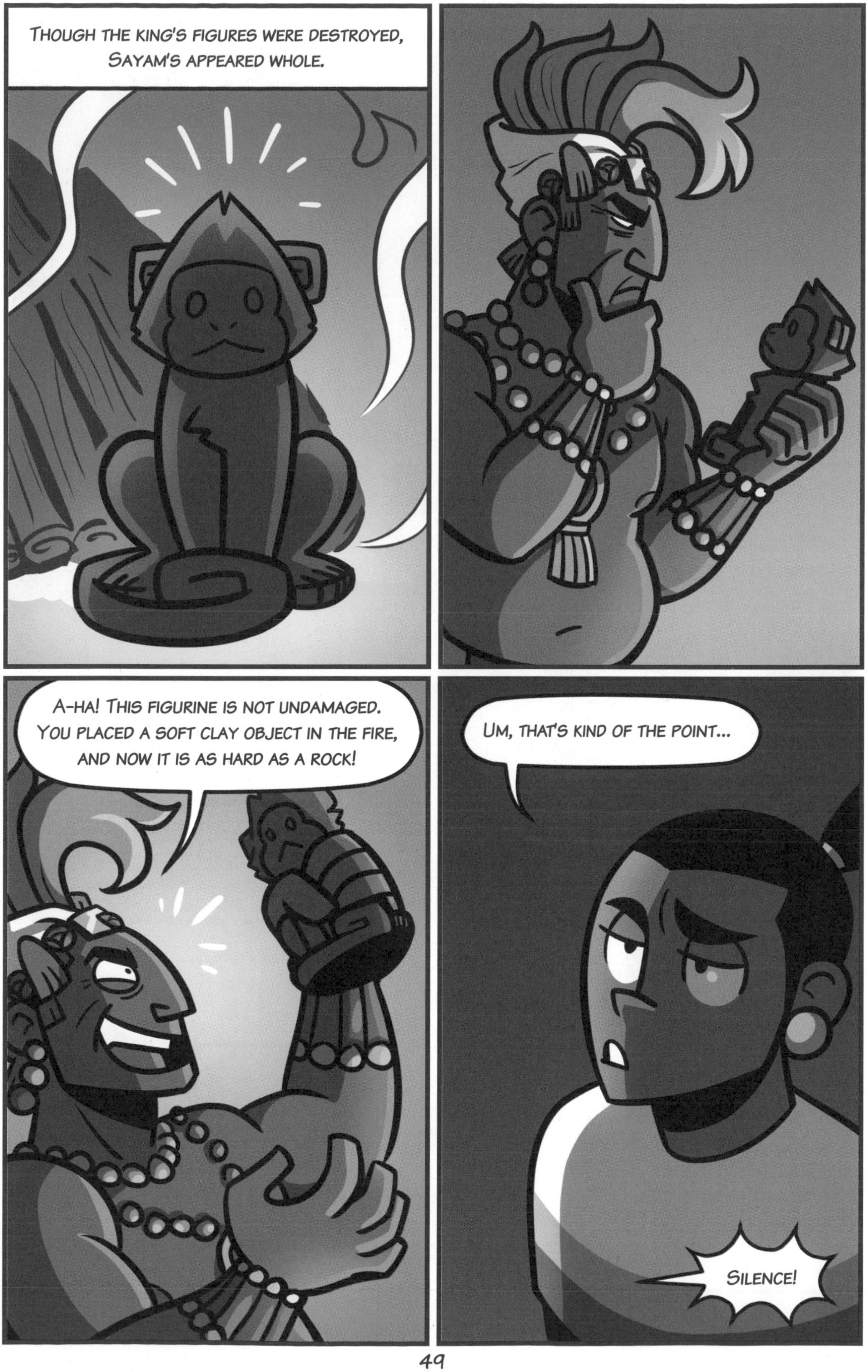
Though the king's figures were destroyed, Sayam's appeared whole.
A-ha! This figurine is not undamaged. You placed a soft clay object in the fire, and now it is as hard as a rock!
Um, that's kind of the point...
Silence!

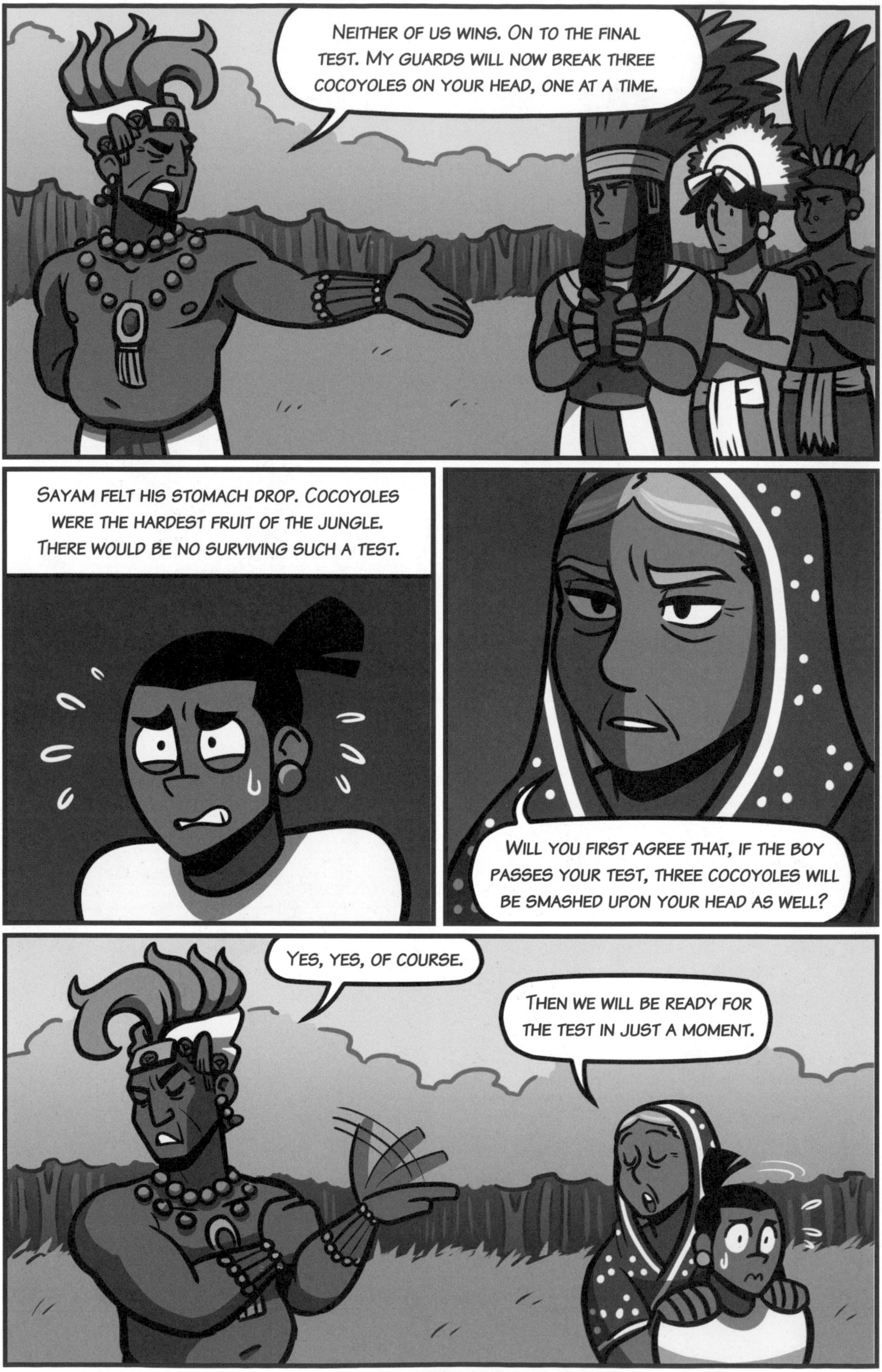

NEITHER OF US WINS. ON TO THE FINAL TEST. MY GUARDS WILL NOW BREAK THREE COCOYOLES ON YOUR HEAD, ONE AT A TIME.
SAYAM FELT HIS STOMACH DROP. COCOYOLES WERE THE HARDEST FRUIT OF THE JUNGLE. THERE WOULD BE NO SURVIVING SUCH A TEST.
WILL YOU FIRST AGREE THAT, IF THE BOY PASSES YOUR TEST, THREE COCOYOLES WILL BE SMASHED UPON YOUR HEAD AS WELL?
YES, YES, OF COURSE.
THEN WE WILL BE READY FOR THE TEST IN JUST A MOMENT.

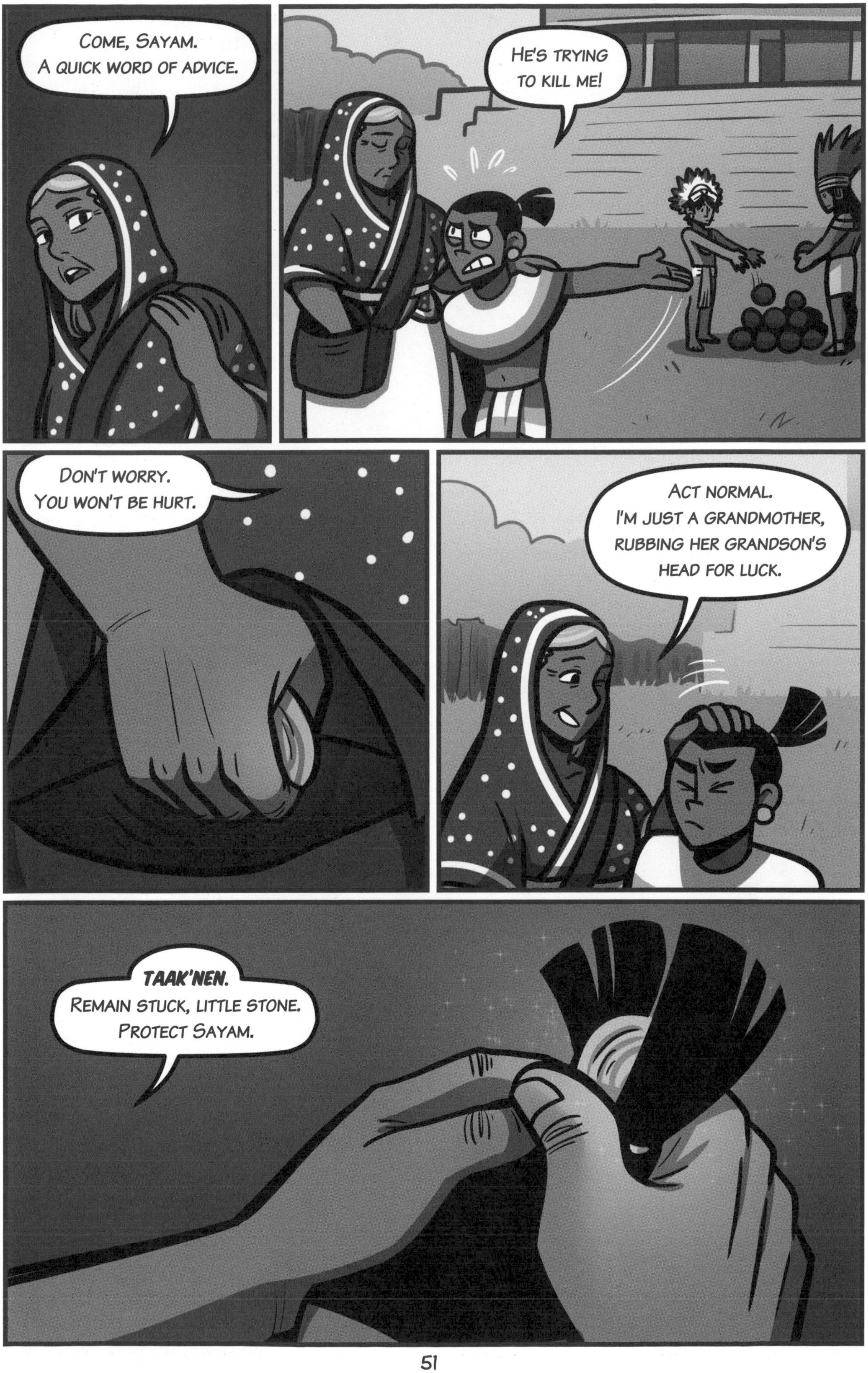
COME, SAYAM.
A QUICK WORD OF ADVICE.
HE'S TRYING TO KILL ME!
DON'T WORRY. YOU WON'T BE HURT.
ACT NORMAL. I'M JUST A GRANDMOTHER, RUBBING HER GRANDSON'S HEAD FOR LUCK.
TAAK'NEN.
REMAIN STUCK, LITTLE STONE. PROTECT SAYAM.

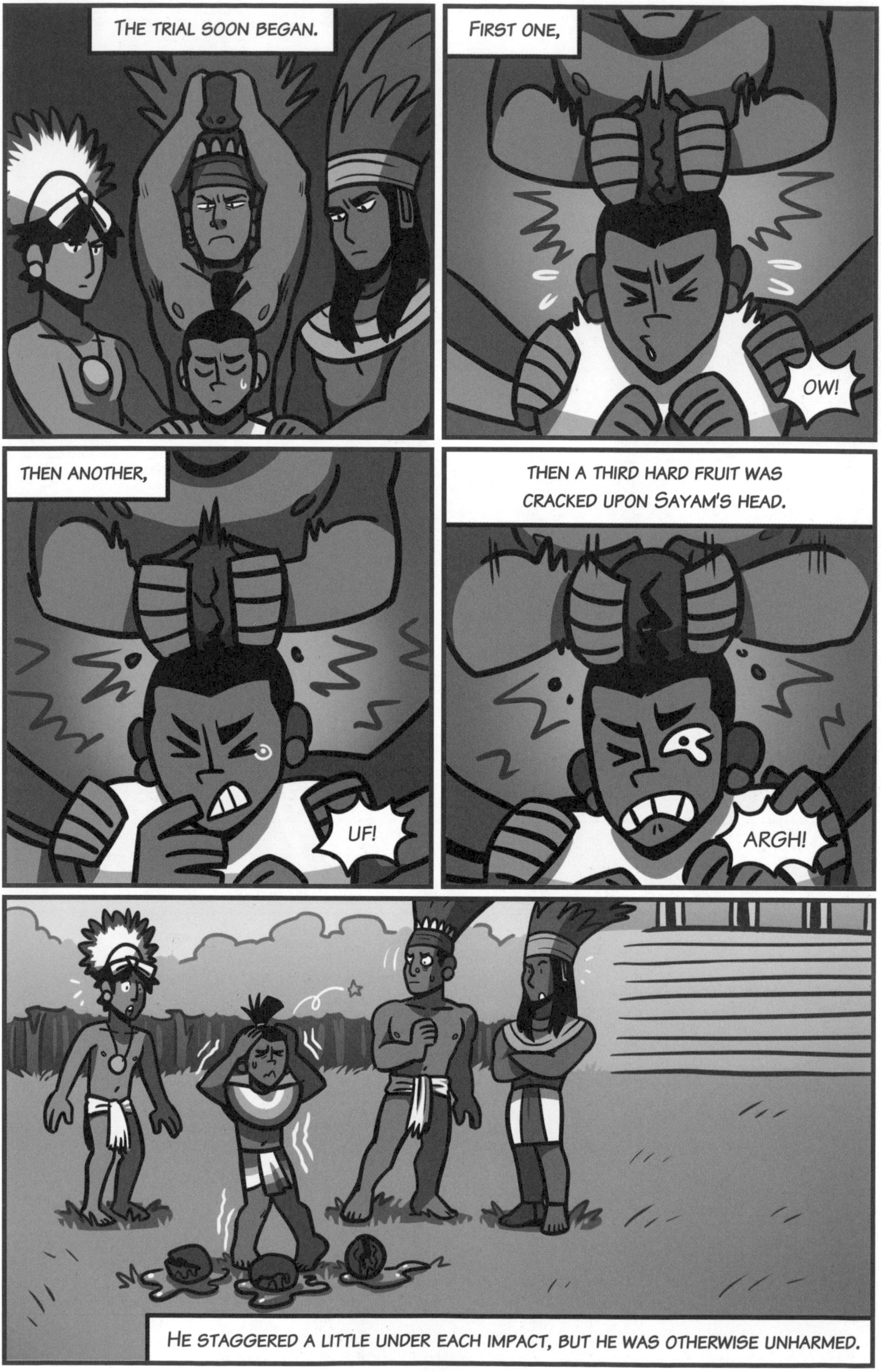
THE TRIAL SOON BEGAN.
FIRST ONE,
OW!
THEN ANOTHER,
UF!
THEN A THIRD HARD FRUIT WAS CRACKED UPON SAYAM'S HEAD.
ARGH!
HE STAGGERED A LITTLE UNDER EACH IMPACT, BUT HE WAS OTHERWISE UNHARMED.

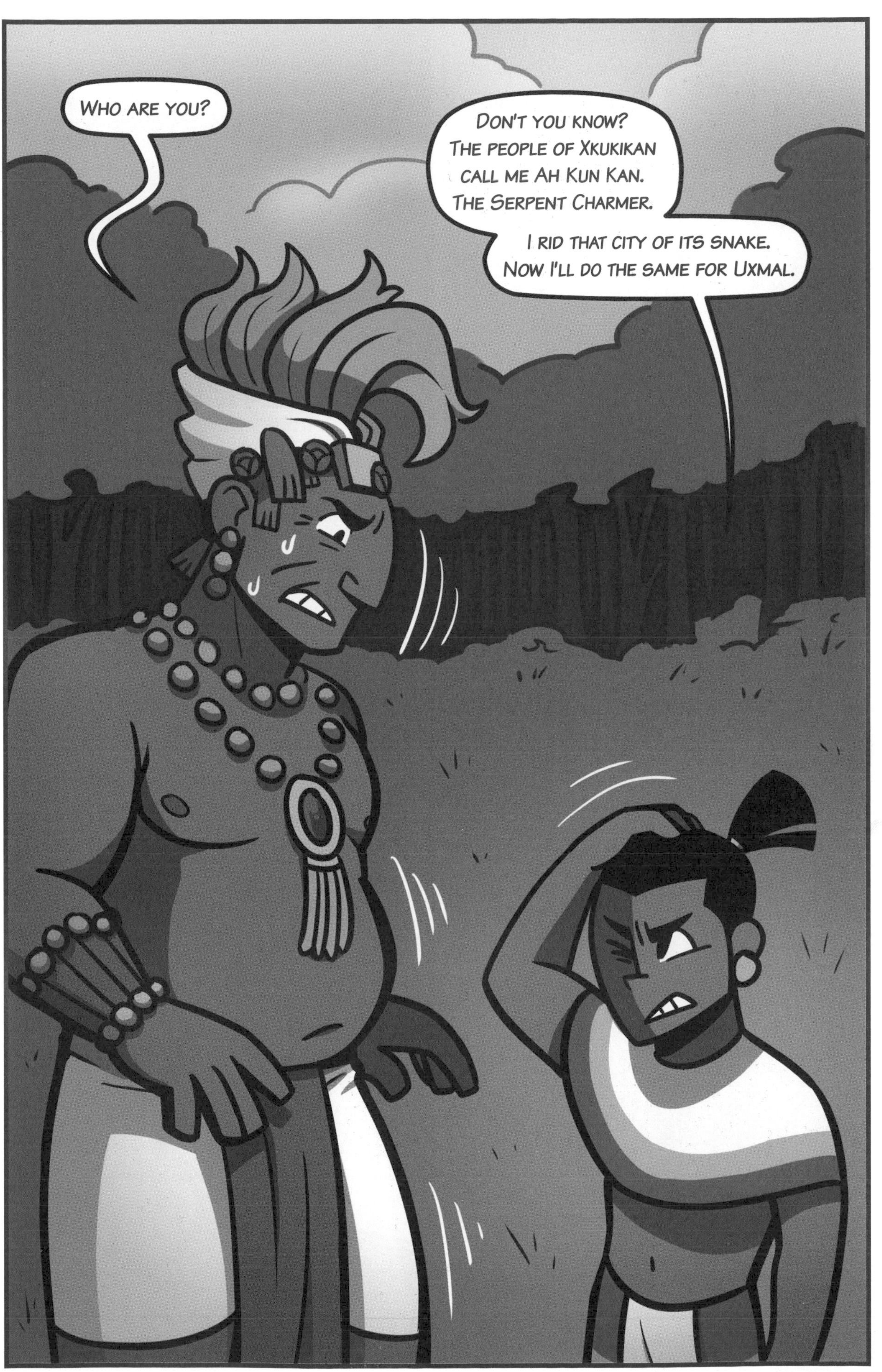
WHO ARE YOU?
DON'T YOU KNOW? THE PEOPLE OF XKUKIKAN CALL ME AH KUN KAN. THE SERPENT CHARMER.
I RID THAT CITY OF ITS SNAKE. NOW I'LL DO THE SAME FOR UXMAL.

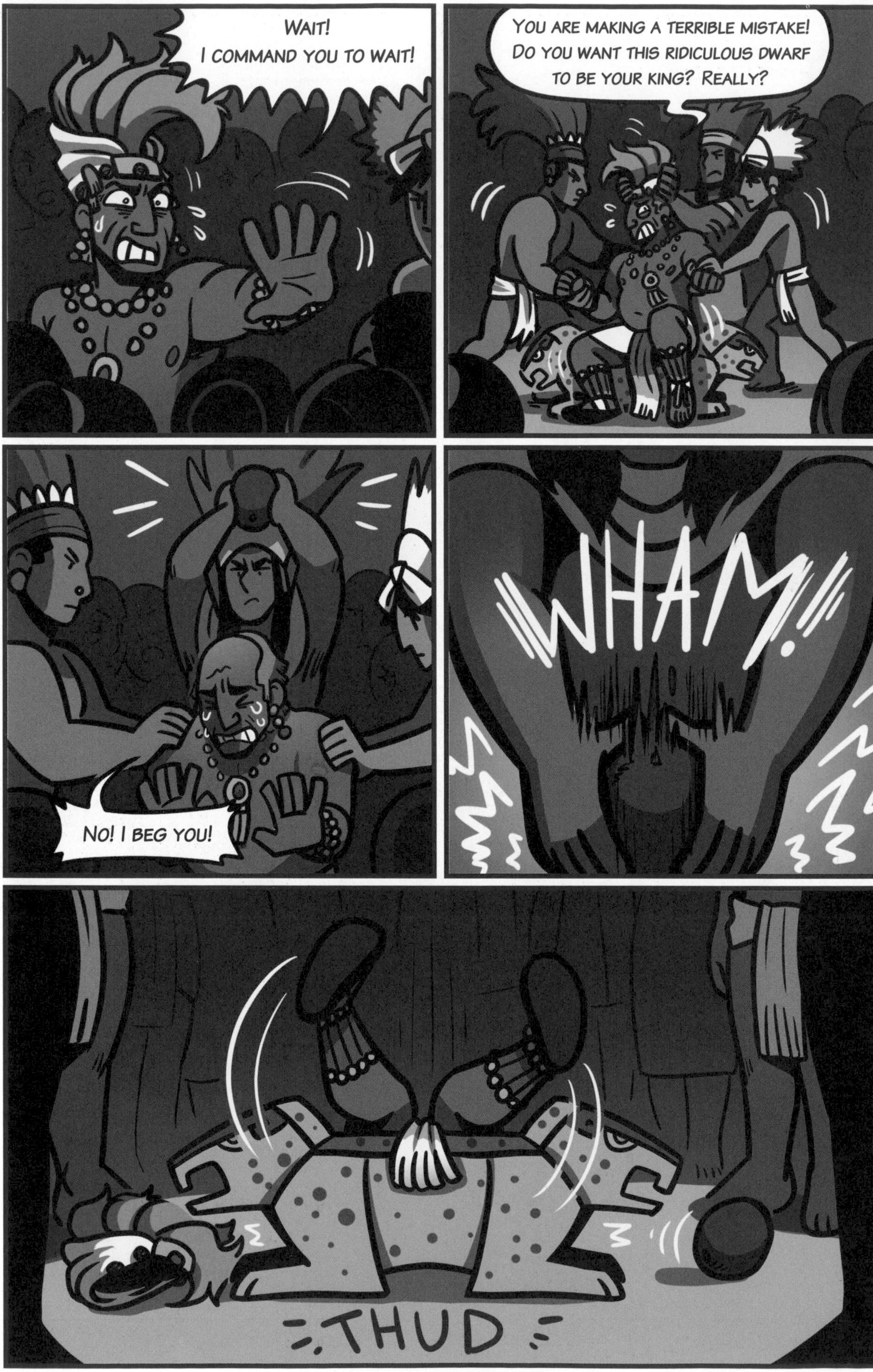
WAIT!
I COMMAND YOU TO WAIT!
YOU ARE MAKING A TERRIBLE MISTAKE! DO YOU WANT THIS RIDICULOUS DWARF TO BE YOUR KING? REALLY?
NO! I BEG YOU!
WHAM!
THUD

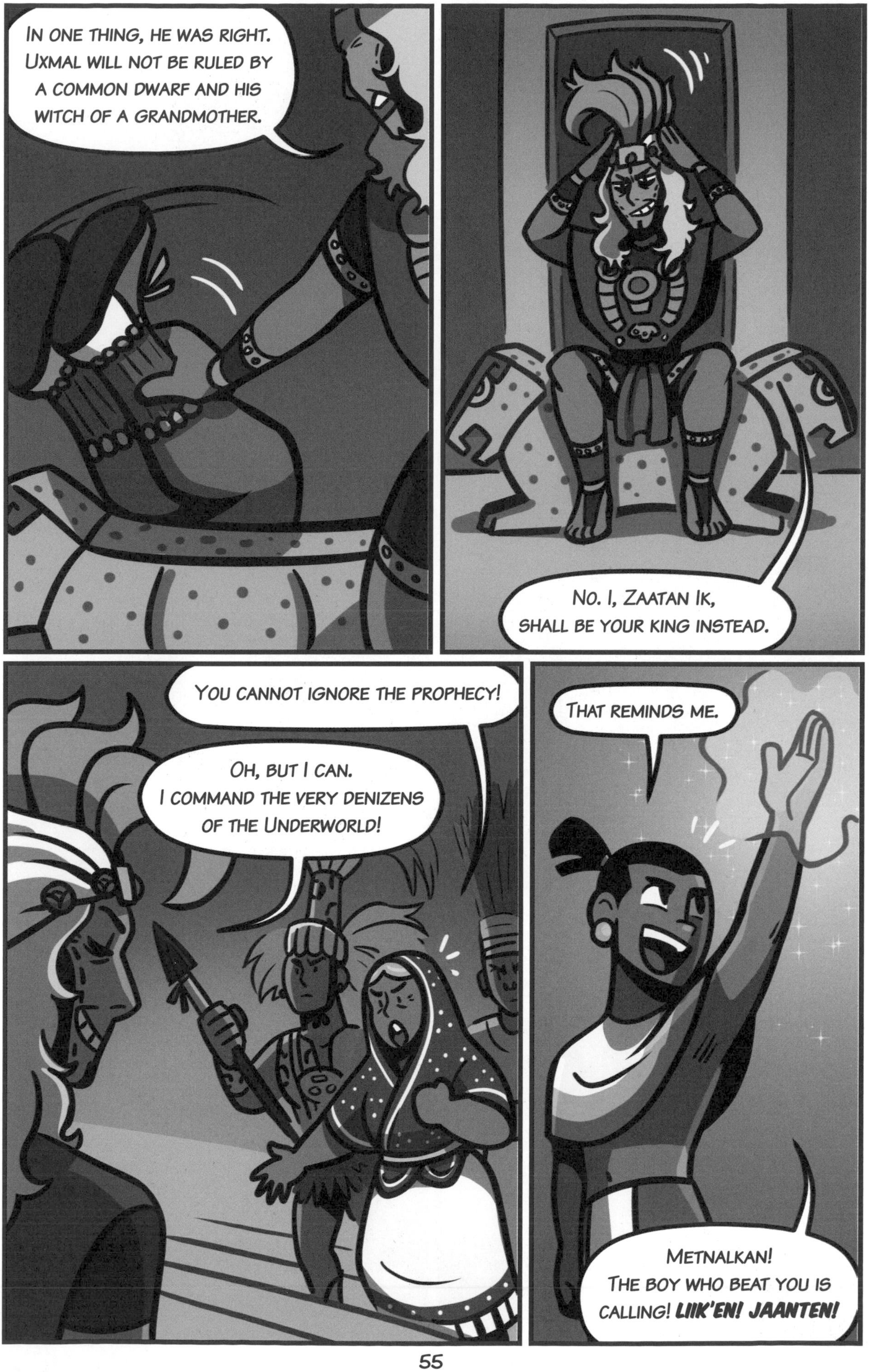
In one thing, he was right. Uxmal will not be ruled by a common dwarf and his witch of a grandmother.
No. I, Zaatan Ik, shall be your king instead.
You cannot ignore the prophecy!
Oh, but I can. I command the very denizens of the Underworld!
That reminds me.
Metnalkan! The boy who beat you is calling! **Liik'en! Jaanten!**

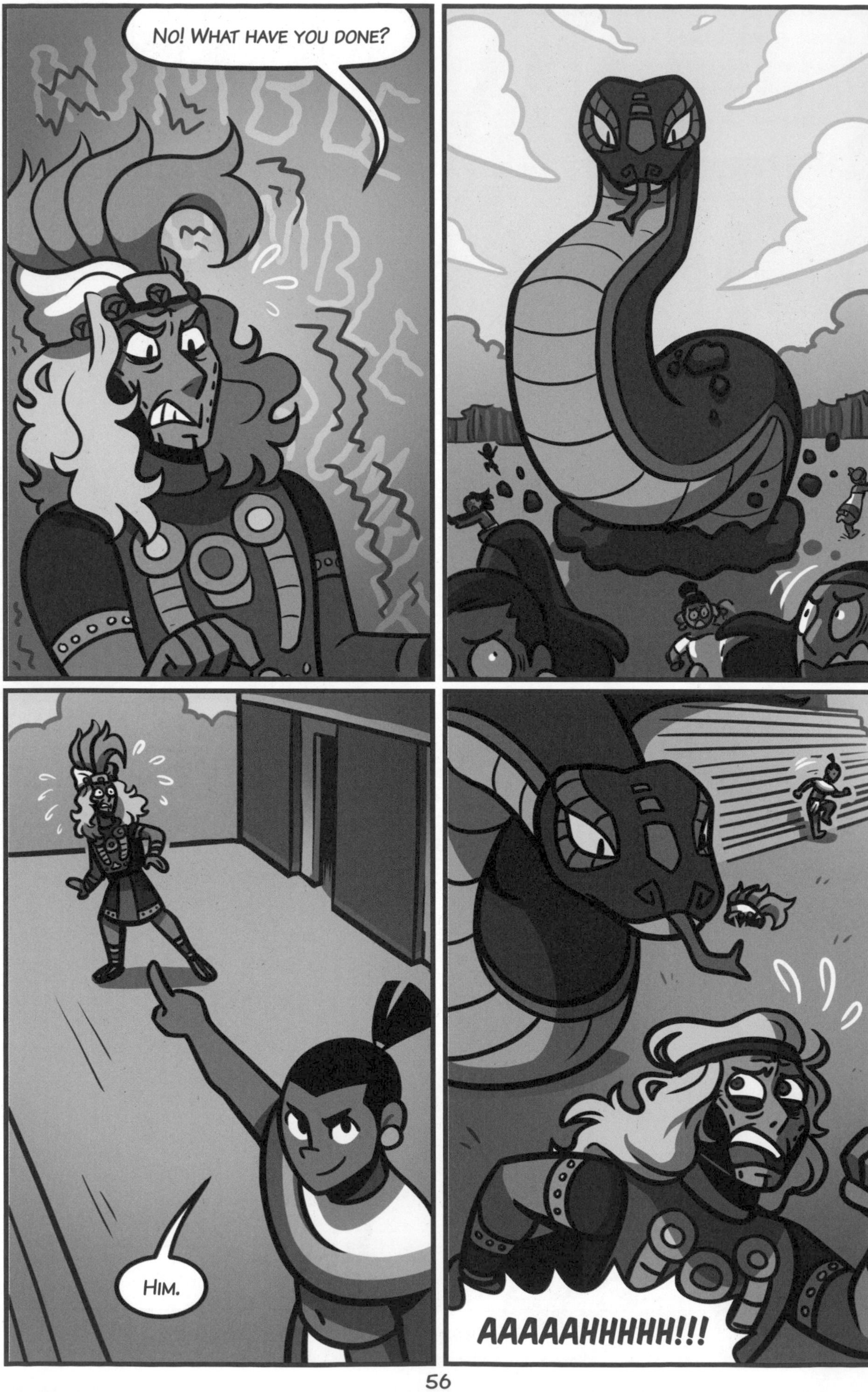
NO! WHAT HAVE YOU DONE?
HIM.
AAAAAHHHHH!!!

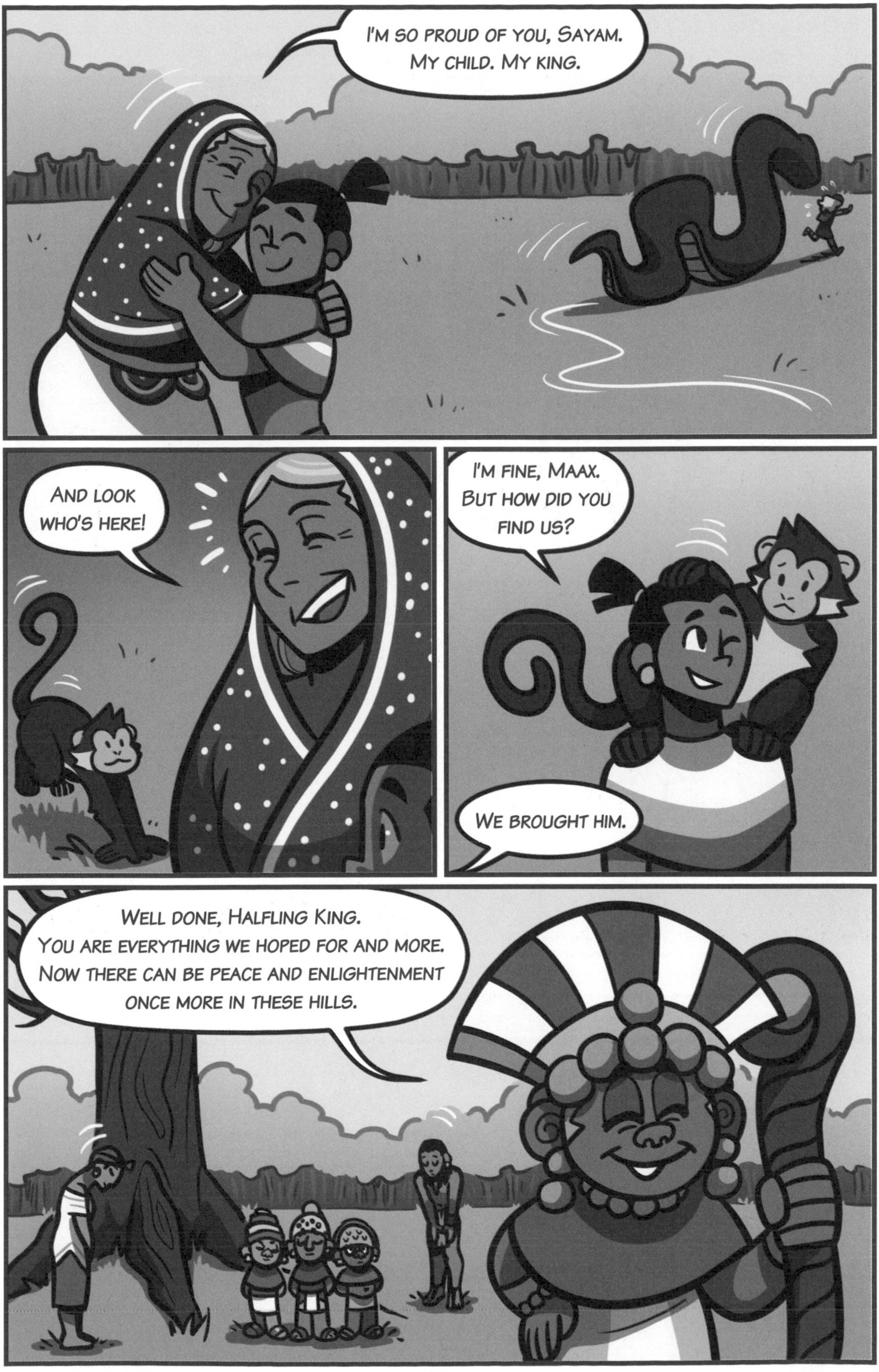
I'M SO PROUD OF YOU, SAYAM.
MY CHILD. MY KING.
AND LOOK WHO'S HERE!
I'M FINE, MAAX. BUT HOW DID YOU FIND US?
WE BROUGHT HIM.
WELL DONE, HALFLING KING. YOU ARE EVERYTHING WE HOPED FOR AND MORE. NOW THERE CAN BE PEACE AND ENLIGHTENMENT ONCE MORE IN THESE HILLS.

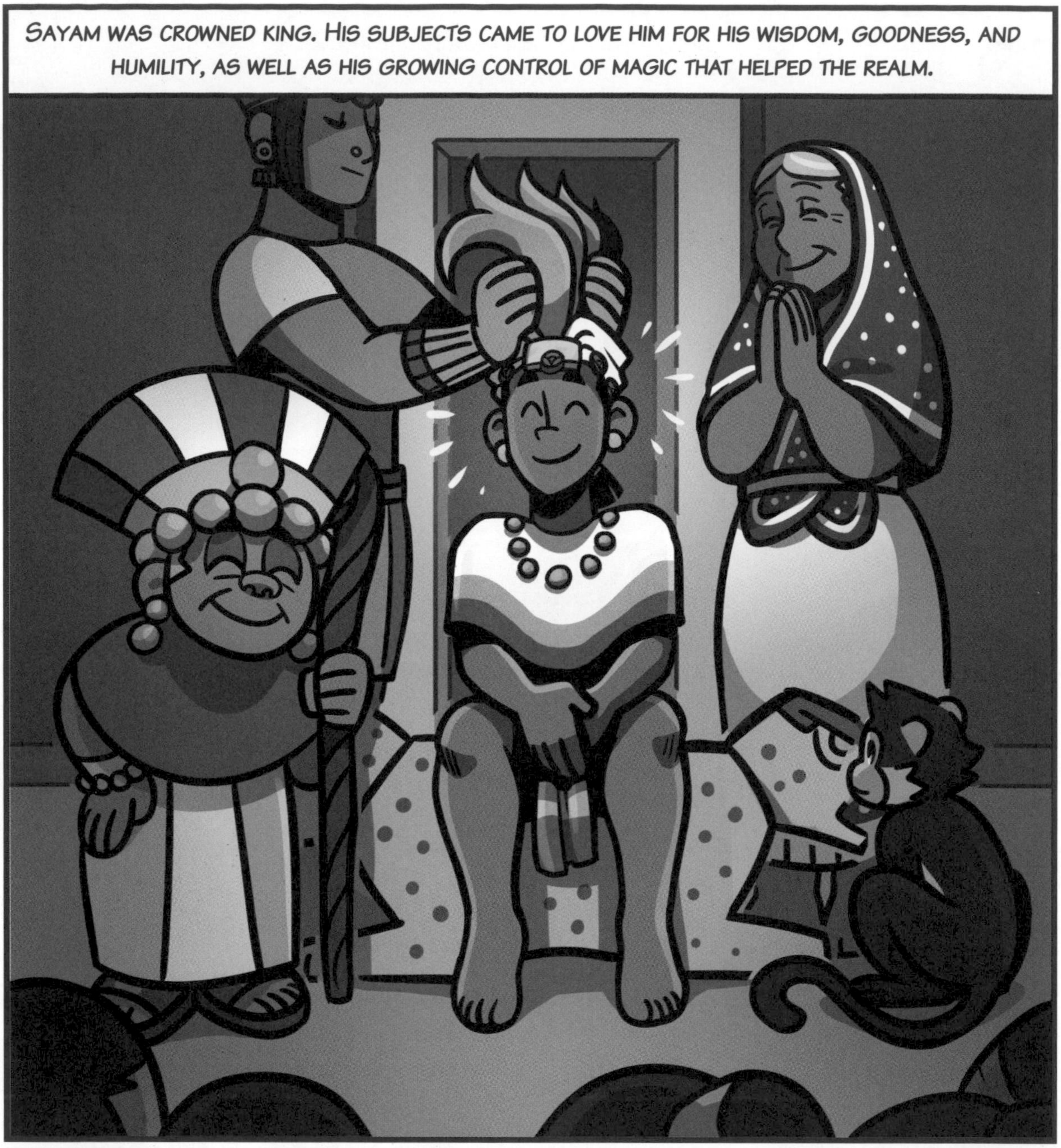
SAYAM WAS CROWNED KING. HIS SUBJECTS CAME TO LOVE HIM FOR HIS WISDOM, GOODNESS, AND HUMILITY, AS WELL AS HIS GROWING CONTROL OF MAGIC THAT HELPED THE REALM.

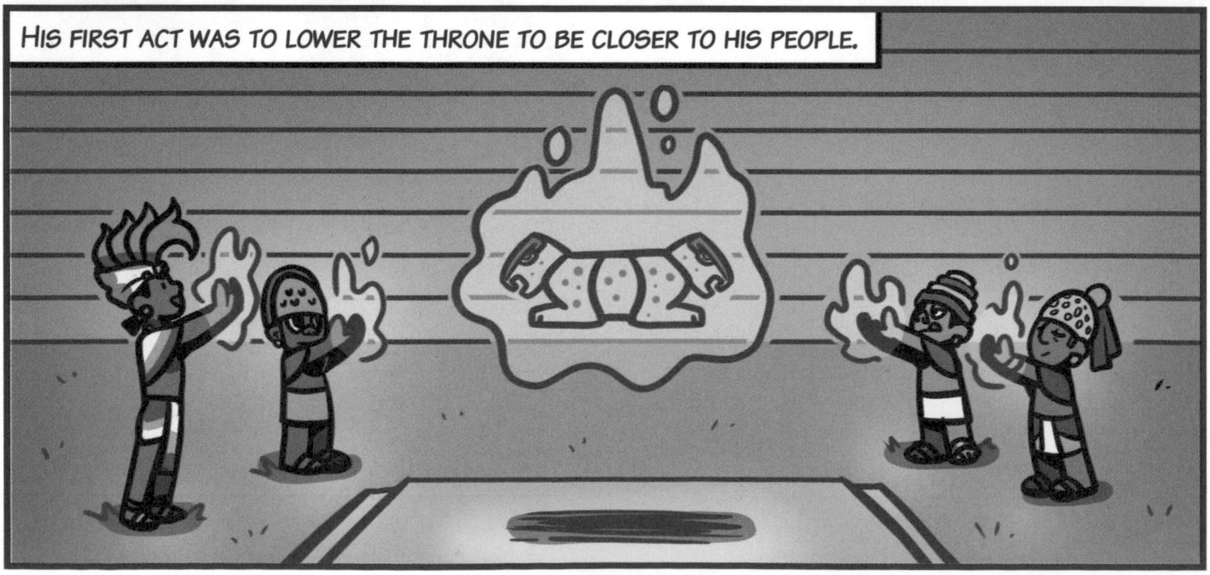
HIS FIRST ACT WAS TO LOWER THE THRONE TO BE CLOSER TO HIS PEOPLE.

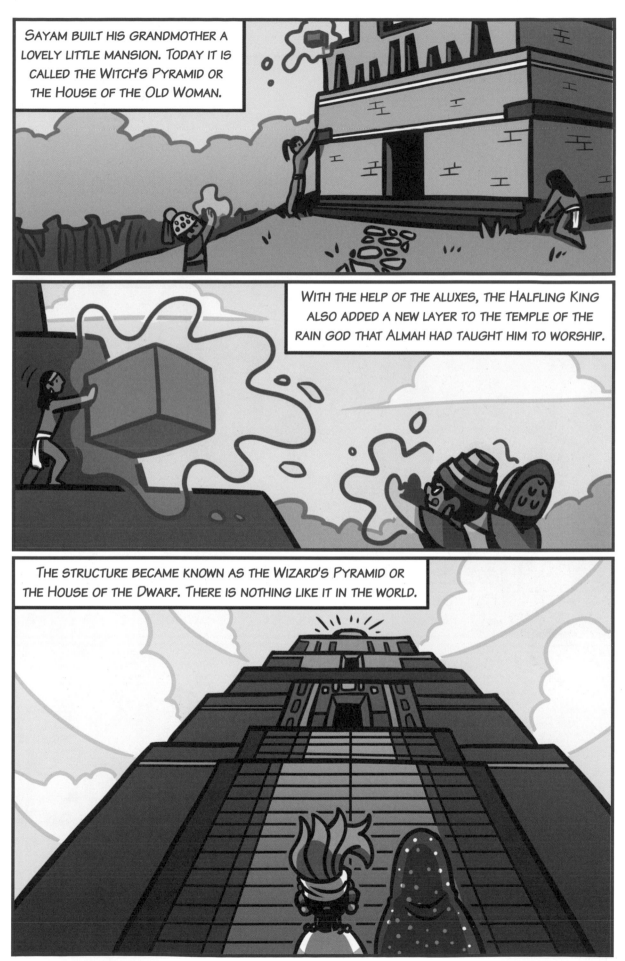

SAYAM BUILT HIS GRANDMOTHER A LOVELY LITTLE MANSION. TODAY IT IS CALLED THE WITCH'S PYRAMID OR THE HOUSE OF THE OLD WOMAN.

WITH THE HELP OF THE ALUXES, THE HALFLING KING ALSO ADDED A NEW LAYER TO THE TEMPLE OF THE RAIN GOD THAT ALMAH HAD TAUGHT HIM TO WORSHIP.

THE STRUCTURE BECAME KNOWN AS THE WIZARD'S PYRAMID OR THE HOUSE OF THE DWARF. THERE IS NOTHING LIKE IT IN THE WORLD.

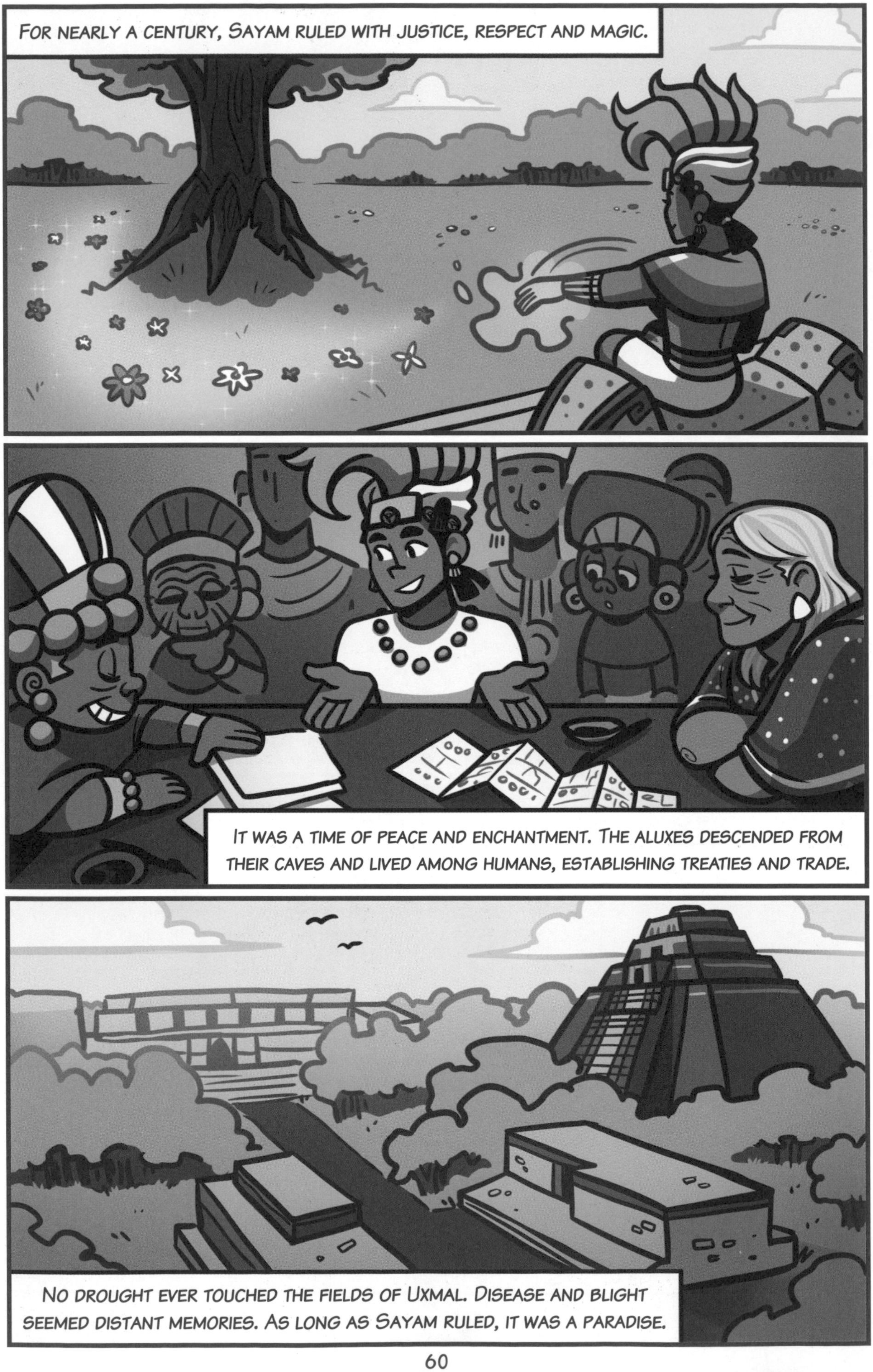
For nearly a century, Sayam ruled with justice, respect and magic.
It was a time of peace and enchantment. The aluxes descended from their caves and lived among humans, establishing treaties and trade.
No drought ever touched the fields of Uxmal. Disease and blight seemed distant memories. As long as Sayam ruled, it was a paradise.

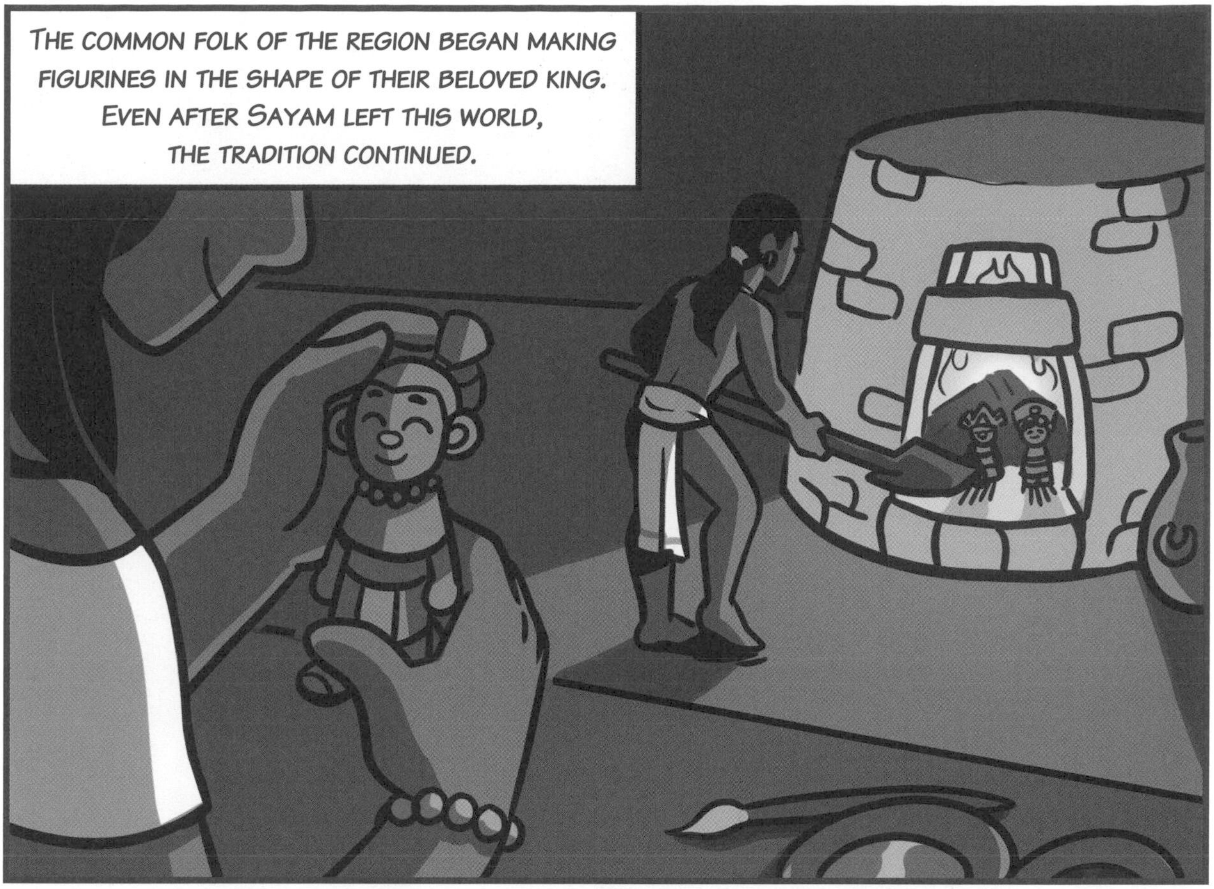
THE COMMON FOLK OF THE REGION BEGAN MAKING FIGURINES IN THE SHAPE OF THEIR BELOVED KING. EVEN AFTER SAYAM LEFT THIS WORLD, THE TRADITION CONTINUED.

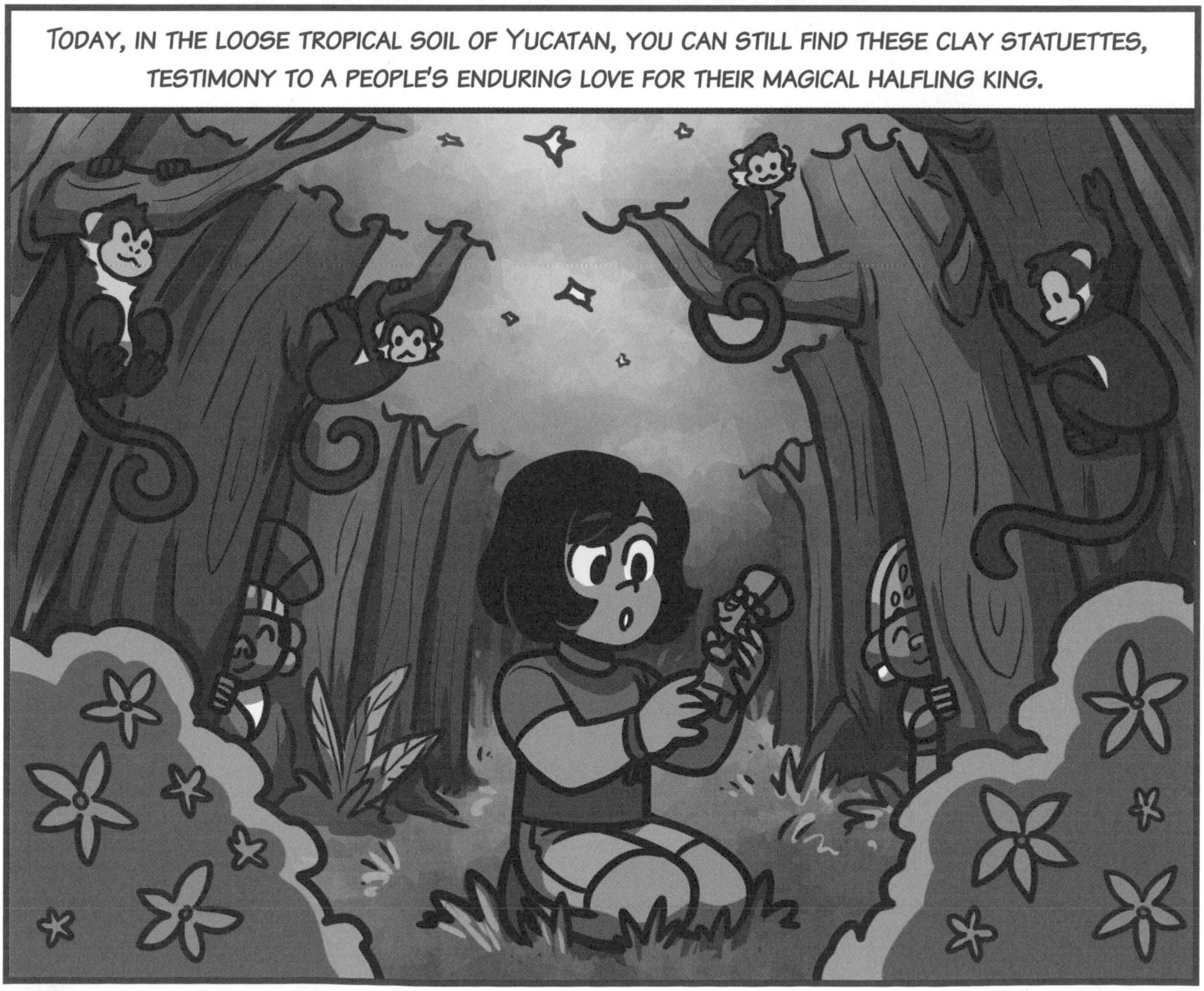
TODAY, IN THE LOOSE TROPICAL SOIL OF YUCATAN, YOU CAN STILL FIND THESE CLAY STATUETTES, TESTIMONY TO A PEOPLE'S ENDURING LOVE FOR THEIR MAGICAL HALFLING KING.

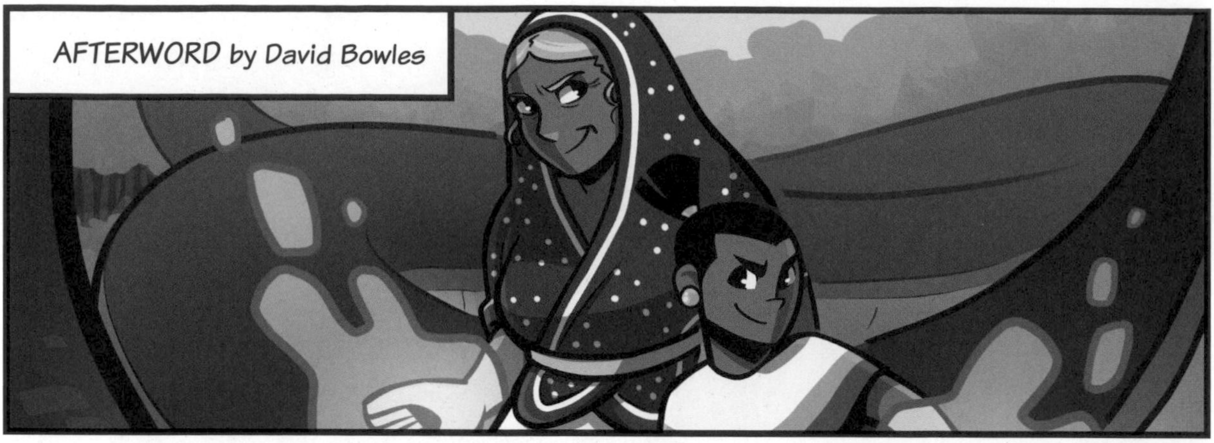
AFTERWORD by David Bowles

At the time of the Spanish Conquest, most indigenous cultures in Mesoamerica preserved their sacred stories and histories with images and a handful of glyphs—icons that represented key names, places, objects. Two thousand years earlier, however, Maya kingdoms had developed an actual writing system based on an elite dialect of the Ch' olti' Mayan language. You can see Sayam the Halfling use those hieroglyphs in the pages of this book as he studies to become a healer like his grandmother.

Time changes things, of course. Fewer and fewer Maya groups could read as centuries passed and the major civilizations collapsed in what's now southern Mexico. Yet the hieroglyphic script was still in use until the Spanish burned most books written with it.

I tell you these facts because when I consider the highly visual way Mesoamericans recorded their stories, the closest modern equivalent that comes to mind is the graphic novel. Blending written words and images, comics and other sorts of graphica allow our brains to process stories more like our ancestors did, using multiple parts of our brains to understand more fully.

You may find this surprising (and perhaps ironic), but grown-ups (yes, even English teachers) are starting to take graphic novels seriously. *The New York Times* recently declared the medium as possibly "the next new literary form." Of course, you and I know that there's nothing new about it. Indigenous people used it for thousands of years.

To honor those folk—whose sacred lore I retranslated and retold in *Feathered Serpent, Dark Heart of Sky*—I have decided at the urging of my editors to collaborate with various illustrators to bring you adaptations of key stories from that book.

The series is called *Tales of the Feathered Serpent*, and it will consist of ten full-color graphic novels full of adventure, humor, beauty, and truth.

I hope that reading the books, you'll find the stories settling deep in your hearts, inspiring you to learn more about the mighty, brilliant, complex peoples of Mesoamerica.

—David Bowles
February 21, 2020

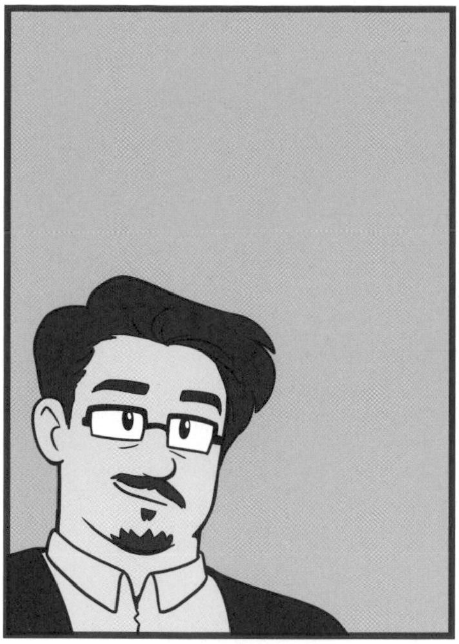

David Bowles is a Mexican American author and educator based in South Texas. He has written fourteen books. His middle grade novel-in-verse *They Call Me Güero* has been the recipient of numerous honors such as the Pura Belpré Honor and the Tomás Rivera Mexican American Children's Book Award, as well as being named to the Bluebonnet Award List.

Charlene Bowles is a comic artist and illustrator living in Texas. She graduated from The University of Texas Rio Grande Valley in 2018. *Rise of the Halfling King* is her debut graphic novel and her work has also been featured on the covers of the award-winning Garza Twins books. She is currently developing many of her own comic projects.

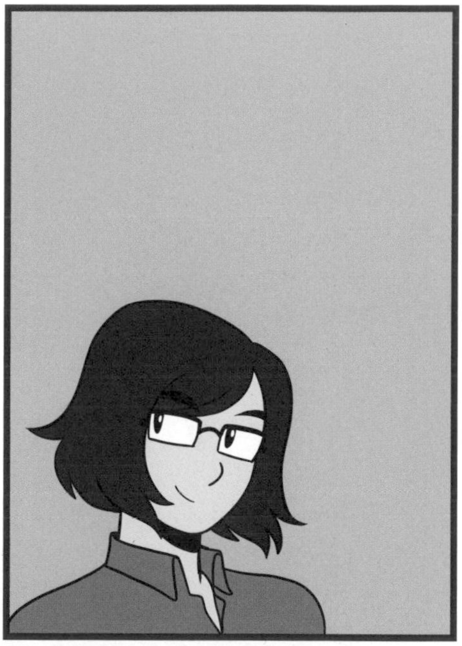

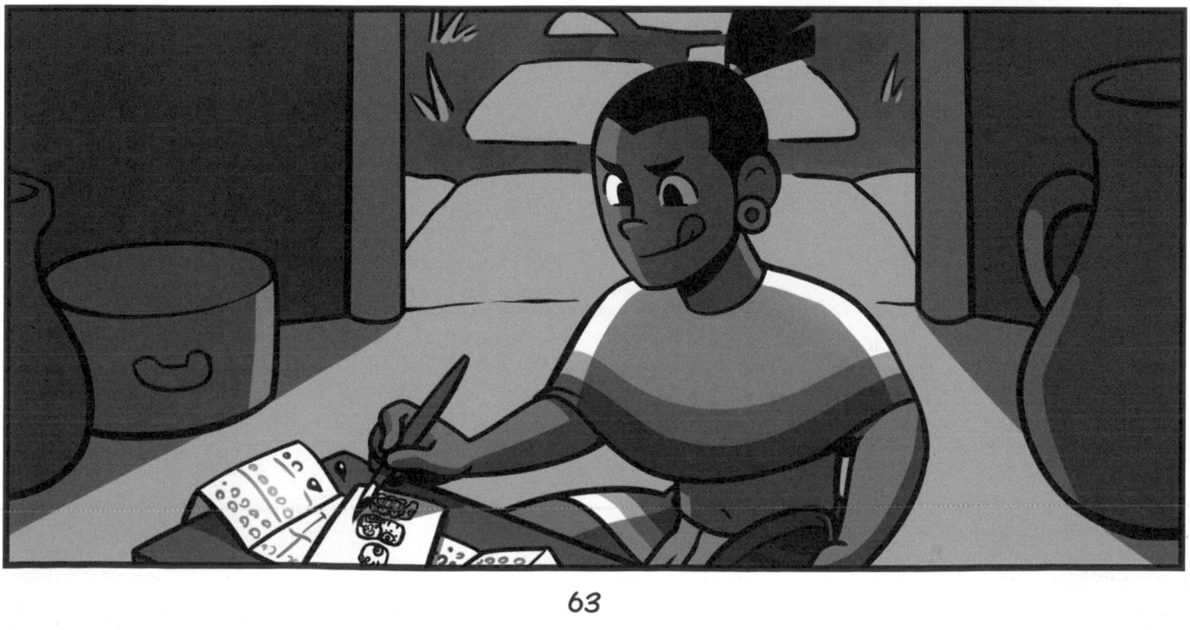

TALES OF THE FEATHERED SERPENT SERIES

This action-packed series will draw from David Bowles' *Feathered Serpent, Dark Heart of Sky* to immerse young readers in some of the legendary tales of ancient Mesoamerican cultures, exploring tales of clever twins who conquer the underworld, star-crossed lovers, women who bravely stand up against conquerors, and more.

Book 2: The Hero Twins in the Realm of Fear

Book 3: Sak Nikte and the Fall of Chichen Itza

Book 4: Princess Hapunda and the Lake

FIRST EDITION
10 9 8 7 6 5 4 3 2 1

Paperback: 978-1-947627-37-6
eBook 978-1-947627-38-3

Library of Congress Cataloging-in-Publication Data

Names: Bowles, David (David O.), author. | Bowles, Charlene, illustrator.
Title: The rise of the halfling king / David Bowles ; illustrated by
    Charlene Bowles.
Description: First edition. | El Paso, Texas : Cinco Puntos Press, [2020] |
    Series: Tales of the feathered serpent ; book 1 | Audience: Grades 7-9.
    | Summary: A magical boy from Mayan mythology faces impossible tasks and
    a ruthless king to save the people of Mexico.
Identifiers: LCCN 2019056170 (print) | LCCN 2019056171 (ebook) | ISBN
    9781947627369 (hardback) | ISBN 9781947627376 (paperback) | ISBN
    9781947627383 (ebook)
Subjects: CYAC: Maya mythology--Fiction. | Magic--Fiction, | Kings, queens,
    rulers, etc.--Fiction. | Adventure and adventures--Fiction. |
    Mexico--Fiction.
Classification: LCC PZ7.7.B68 Ri 2021 (print) | LCC PZ7.7.B68 (ebook) |
    DDC 741.5/973--dc23
LC record available at https://lccn.loc.gov/2019056170
LC ebook record available at https://lccn.loc.gov/2019056171

VISIT CINCOPUNTOS.COM FOR MORE INFORMATION